I0553414

Masks

A 1Night Stand Anthology

By

Dakota Trace

This book is a work of fiction. Names, characters, places, and incidents are the products of the author's imagination or used fictitiously. Any resemblance to actual events, locales or persons, living or dead, is entirely coincidental.

Copyright © 2016 by Dakota Trace
ISBN: 978-1-68361-057-1
Cover art by Dakota Trace

All rights reserved. Except for use in any review, the reproduction or utilization of this work, in whole or in part, in any form by any electronic, mechanical or other means now known or hereafter invented, is forbidden without the written permission of the publisher.

Published by Decadent Publishing Company, LLC
Look for us online at:
www.decadentpublishing.com

Blind Need

Two wounded souls, one blind and the other scarred, are matched up by the famous Madame Evangeline— neither one expecting more than a brief meeting of two bodies in the dark for one night.

Xaviera Navarro had it all, a wonderful career ahead of her running her family's wine business, a sexy fiancé, and her dream-wedding around the corner, but that all changed in the blink of an eye. A freak accident has left the Navarro wine heiress blind with no future other than the company of her seeing-eye dog, Lucy. After licking her wounds, she finally is tired of her own company and ventures out in hopes of finding a man who might be strong enough to stand beside her but not in front of her. If she can't have that, she'll settle for a night of hot loving before returning home.

Ignatius "Nate" Ramirez is not only a scarred fire-jumper with a justifiably bad attitude toward women, he's also under strict orders by his Captain that if he doesn't get laid on his vacation, he's going to bench him. After finding out about 1Night Stand, he requests Madame Evangeline find him the perfect fantasy woman to have under the cover of darkness. Figuring he'll have a better chance with his date with all the lights out, he wasn't expecting a feisty, no punches pulled heiress to knock him off his feet.

A blind woman and a scarred fire-jumper should be a match made in heaven, but will Nate and Xaviera manage to leave their baggage at the door and find love all in one night.
Blurb

Chapter One

"We're here, Ms. Navarro." The car glided to a stop.

"Thank you, Carlos." Xaviera patted the seat beside her for her purse. As usual, it seemed to have slipped away from her side during the drive. *There isn't anybody to blame but myself for it escaping again. I should've realized seven hours is too long to hold onto even a small purse.* A cold nose touched her hand. A reluctant grin tugged at her lips as a wet mouth closed around her wrist, guiding it until her fingers brushed leather. *My faithful companion—they broke the mold when they made you, baby.*

"I feel it, Lucy." The black lab's mouth left her. She didn't know what she'd have done after the freak car malfunction that had taken her sight if her parents hadn't gotten her Lucy. *She's a godsend.* Hearing the click of the door handle, she slid forward and waited for Carlos to speak.

"Step out, Ms. Navarro. The curb is approximately ten inches away." Listening to his advice, she put her hand out; thankful her handyman's wife hadn't thrown a fit when she'd asked him to drive her to Vegas this weekend. She'd lucked out. He planned to stay at his son's place to visit his grandkids while she was on her date. He'd only be a phone call away if she needed him. And there was no other man she trusted as much. *Thank God, María is a romantic soul. I wonder what she'd say if she realized this is a one-night stand?* 1Night Stand was a last ditch effort on her part to find a man for at least a night before she swore off them altogether.

Madame Evangeline had promised not only the highest discretion, but also guaranteed that all potential dates would have a thorough background check. And Lord knew she needed privacy after the fiasco of her accident, followed by her prestigious fiancé dumping her. Men had crawled out of the woodwork once the news hit that the newly-blind Navarro heiress was available. *I'm sick of men who either want my money or worse only want to take care of me. I'm blind—not an invalid.* Paired with the idea of being able to have one glorious night of sexual release before parting ways with the man, 1NS was a dream come true for a woman like her. She only hoped Madame Evangeline came through with what her high-end matchmaking site promised.

"Steady, miss."

Hanging onto Carlos's hand, she allowed him to guide her out of the car. A moment later, Lucy's harness handle brushed her palm. Wrapping her hand around it, she took a deep breath, listening intently to the ambient noises. The sounds most took for granted were her lifeline. She heard the chatter of a group of people walking by, the softer sound of a door opening, the jangling of slot machines, then silence as the door closed. *I must be close to the front door of the casino.* After receiving her instructions about her date, she'd gone online to see what amenities the flagship of Castillo Resorts had to offer. *Just in case I get stood up.*

"The door is ahead of you, ten feet, and at two o'clock." Carlos released her hand then paused. His silence was heavy.

She sighed. *Protective, as always.* "What is it?"

"Are you sure you want to do this?" The question didn't surprise her, nor did its gruffness. "The missus has a very rosy view, but I know why you are here."

Her cheeks warmed. Carlos had been with her family long before her accident, one of the most trusted workers on Father's vineyard. As a beloved grandfather figure to her, the last thing she wanted to talk to him about was her sex life—or her lack of one. "A woman has needs, too. I'm tired of being alone. This is a safe way to get my feet wet again." There was no way she would admit to her true motives because she couldn't chance him packing her and Lucy back into the car then driving her non-stop all the way home.

"Of course it is, *mi nieta.*" He pressed a kiss against her temple. "I'll be back for you tomorrow around one. Can you find the front desk all right?"

Pursing her lips, she shook her head. "How many times do I have to tell you, I'm blind, not helpless?" Lifting to her toes, she kissed the air where she assumed his face was. A moment later her lips touched the sandpapery skin of his cheek. "But I do thank you for the ride. Now, scoot before María wonders where you are. Didn't you tell her you would call her from your son's?"

"Yes, I did." He wrapped a hand around her arm. "Call me if you need me, Xaviera. I'm not kidding."

She forced a laugh. "I will, but everything will be fine. You'll see."

As he released her, she only hoped her words were true.

***

Sitting in the semi-lit hotel room, Ignatius Ramirez-Santiago once again wondered why he had come. He didn't know how he'd let his smokejumper captain talk him into this cockamamie idea or paying for the ridiculously high-priced suite. *Well maybe the, "you don't get your ass laid while you're on vacation, I'm benching you," was what did it. I wish it was only that simple.* Eying the wide bed, he wondered if he could go through with making love to a woman he barely knew. Sure his cock was more than ready to have its yearlong celibacy broken, but *he* wasn't. *My cock doesn't have to deal with a cringing lover when she realizes how fucked up I am. That's why this date with 1Night Stand is ideal. I won't have to explain how my dumb ass got burned trying to help put out a canyon fire.* He'd filled out the stupid survey Madame Evangeline emailed him in hopes of finding his fantasy fuck and she'd delivered. *Or so she claimed.* His date still hadn't shown.

He didn't know much about the woman 1Night Stand had paired him with other than her willingness to go along with his groping-in-the-dark scenario. Before his accident he'd been the type of lover who detested screwing with the lights off. A visual creature, he wanted—no, he needed to see every emotion cross his lover's face. *Amazing what a few scars will do to that.* He hadn't thought the scars along his neck and down his left shoulder were all that bad. He'd seen much worse in the burn unit at the hospital, but his lovers proclaimed otherwise. These days he'd settle for temporary release—just enough to take the edge off. *Maybe a whole night of fucking will get me back on track for a while.* The brisk knock on the door just before the spill of light from the hallway jerked him out of his thoughts. His shoulders tensed, his attention glued to the shadowy figure. *Was it her? The man at desk had assured him she would have a key to his room.*

"Mr. Ramirez-Santiago?" The outline of what only could be a man appeared in the block of illumination. His shoulders slumped even while a bit of unease filled him. *Who the hell is that?*

"Yeah." His response came out much rougher than he intended and the person flinched. Now that the guy had entered farther into the room, Nate recognized the front desk manager from his earlier check-in.

"Your date...."

He clenched his fists around the slender, wooden arms of his chair. They creaked ominously. "She cancelled didn't she?" *Fuck! What the hell do I do?*

"No, sir." The man shifted from foot to foot. "She's been unavoidably delayed. There was a minor accident in the lobby and Ms. Navarro would like a chance to refresh herself before joining you."

***

"I'm so sorry, Ms. Navarro!" The harried voice of the female hotel attendant almost cut through the fury flowing through her veins. Wet from her impromptu dip, she accepted the terry cloth towel pressed into her hands. *Whose genius idea was it to put a damn fountain in the middle of a lobby? And why does this always seem to happen to me? Do I need to hang a sign around my neck that says "I'm blind, please don't stand so close you accidentally*

9

knock me over."

"She's a hazard!" The nasal whine from her attacker set her nerves on edge. Dropping the towel on the arm of the chair she sat in, she prayed for patience. "Dogs aren't allowed at Castillo Resorts—"

"There is no such rule, ma'am. We're a pet-friendly resort, and even if we weren't—" Whatever else the hotel concierge was trying to say was lost as the woman continued her tirade.

"I want to report her to the manager. This is an outrage. She should be thrown out!" Her tone faded a bit and Xaviera knew the employee must've stepped between her and her assailant. "I have reserved one of the best suites this hotel has to offer. I've been coming to Castillo Resorts for the past ten years because they don't allow animals in the buildings. Dander irritates my allergies. What gives *her* the right to flaunt the rules?" The clack of the woman stomping her foot rang through the lobby.

"I'm not breaking any of them, but even if there were one which stated no dogs, the fact that I'm blind would trump it." Gritting her teeth, she rubbed the towel through her wet hair. "She's a seeing eye dog—a service animal, and federal law states I'm allowed to take her everywhere with me. If you had watched where you were going, you wouldn't have stepped on her or knocked me into the fountain." The sound of Lucy's pain-filled yelp before she fell into the water echoed in her ears. Anxious to check her dog, she snapped her fingers, the signal to come. As soon as the furry body pressed close, she ran her palms over Lucy's legs, feeling for injuries.

"Well, I never!" The irate woman paused. "Thank God you've come!" The noise of shuffling feet and rat-a-tat of heels had Xaviera thinking the manager had finally arrived. "Please explain to this...woman that she needs to take her dog and leave before my eyes swell shut." Her voice trembled. Xaviera was stunned. *Is she actually crying? What the hell? Just a second ago she was acting like a real fishwife.*

"I'm not sure who informed you there were no animals allowed at Castillo Resorts, but they were wrong. We have always been pro-animal. I'm sorry if the dander bothers your allergies, but I cannot and will not ban a seeing eye dog."

"You're taking *her* side?" The fishwife was back.

"Ma'am, I'm sorry but the guide dog stays. You can either check out or have Linda escort you to the bar for a complimentary drink to calm your nerves after this...accident. Either way, Ms. Navarro and her companion are staying." The calmness radiating from the male set her at ease despite not being able to see. *I hope this means I can go to my room and change out of these wet clothes before my date decides I've stood him up.* Relaxing against the chair, she listened to the woman's shrill voice fade as Linda led her away.

"I'm sorry about this, Mr...?" She waited for him to supply the name.

"Castillo. Jackson Castillo. But it is I who am sorry for this situation, Ms. Navarro. When Eve told me you would be coming and the special circumstances, I planned on seeing you settled myself. An issue came up in my meeting and delayed me. So please accept my apology for not being here to greet you."

A frown tugged at her lips as she stood. "Sir, I expect to be treated the same as your other guests. I don't expect any special attention nor should my family name affect...."

A hand wrapped around her elbow while the scent of expensive cologne teased her nostrils. "And it doesn't. But setting up a blind date for a blind woman requires special attention, don't you agree? Imagine how Eve would feel if you ended up in the wrong place by mistake. I planned on merely making sure you found your suite along with the room where your...date is to happen, without issues. Please let me assure you, your family name has nothing to do with the matter."

Cocking her head, she tried to determine his sincerity. Being able to visually determine sincerity was one of the many things she missed since her accident. At her hip, her cell vibrated. It had somehow managed to survive her dunk in the water. Stopping, she retrieved it from the clip on her jeans. Feeling for the correct key, she pressed it.

"You have one new text," the disembodied voice reported. "Press one to retrieve new text." Sliding her fingers across the keys, she did. "New text, received at 5:32 p.m., from 1Night Stand. I hope you found Jackson to be helpful. Please enjoy your evening. Don't do anything I wouldn't. Madame Evangeline. End Message." Her face flushed as she snapped the phone shut. "It's obvious your partner knows you well, Mr. Castillo."

"I have nothing to do with the 1Night Stand, Ms. Navarro, other than providing the accommodations...and please call me Jackson." He sounded relieved.

I wonder why? "Of course, Jackson." She snapped her fingers once more. The handle of Lucy's harness brushed their tips. Grabbing hold, she gave him a smile. Or at least she hoped she smiled at him and not off into space. "Now, if you can lead me to my hotel room, I would love to get out of these wet clothes before my date decides I've cancelled on him."

"Of course, and don't worry, I had an employee let Mr. Ramirez-Santiago know there's been an unavoidable delay. I'm sure he'll be most understanding." There was a pause. "Daniel, please carry Ms. Navarro's bag up to her room."

"Yes, Jackson." The rustle of her luggage and the brush of a body told her the bellhop scurried to do his duty.

"Shall we?" he asked.

Taking a deep breath, she agreed. "Lead the way."

Chapter Two

I f not feeling a bit more refreshed when she stepped out of her room, Xaviera was a least much drier than she had been when she'd entered. Behind the closed door, Lucy whined. "I'll be back later, girl. Be good." Realizing it wasn't the safest choice, she still left the dog behind. *This date's about having my itch scratched—to find out if sex is still as good as I remember. Nothing more, nothing less. Taking Lucy more than likely will freak out my date.* A soft exhale reached her ears. "Jackson?"

"You're beautiful, Xaviera." She turned to the left, where she judged him to be. "Your dress is the epitome of sexiness. Light and airy, it's every man's visual fantasy."

Smoothing her hands over the cotton sundress, she nibbled on her lower lip. "Are you sure? I can imagine you're more familiar with silk and saffron, than cotton and vanilla."

His fingers brushed her bare arm. "I pride myself on my acquaintance with both. I am a man first and foremost. If I say your date will not be disappointed, it's the truth."

Taking a deep breath, she took a step toward him. "No need to twist my arm. I'll take your word." *Besides, it won't matter because he'll never actually set eyes on me. Anonymity is the keyword for this meeting*. She sobered, remembering the email where Madame Evangeline had assured her that her prospective date wanted the fantasy or illusion of his lover never being able to see his face. *Something I can deliver*. Pushing her morbid thoughts away, she offered her arm. "If you'd be so kind as to guide me in the right direction, I'd like to find out if my date will approve as you have."

Counting the steps in her head, she was surprised at how close her date's room was to hers. *He's been right next door the whole time*. "You've thought ahead. It's very helpful, putting us next to each other—I think even I can manage this short distance without a guide."

"I believe in giving the best service to all my customers, both sighted and unsighted guests...."

The rattle of an approaching cart caught her attention. "Housekeeping or room service?"

"Quite astute of you. I've taken the liberty of ordering a light repast for you and your date."

"Thank you again, I'm sure he'll be most grateful for the food afterward."

There was a pause. "I'm certain." A click followed by the sound of the door handle being turned caught her attention. "There you are. The cart will remain in the hall until needed." He guided her over the threshold. "This room is set up identical to yours. Have a pleasant night." His hand left her elbow. "If you need anything at all, please don't hesitate to call."

"I won't." Stepping forward with a bravado she didn't feel, she let the door close behind her with a subtle thud. From her right came a masculine voice. "Finally, my date has arrived."

Cocking her head, she nodded before remembering he probably couldn't see her. "Yes. I apologize for the delay. It was unavoidable." Taking a tentative step forward, she used her fingertips to guide her along the short entryway into the main area of the suite. *If it's like my room, there should be ten paces until I reach the chair sitting at three o'clock from the bed.* Counting the steps, she was surprised when her hand didn't encounter anything but empty air. She stopped, unwilling to embarrass herself by tripping over the missing piece of furniture.

"Hmmm, no chair. Did you rearrange the room, Mr. Ramirez-Santiago?"

Nate's eyes devoured the lush figure of the woman standing not ten feet from him. The dim light spilling from the lamp behind her outlined every curve and dip. His hands itched to touch her. He stifled his moan as his cock swelled behind the placket of his khaki shorts. It was all he could do to stay seated. Clearing his throat, he focused on getting his raging libido under control. *Get a grip, Nate. One-night stand or not, she's not expecting to be jumped the second she enters the room.* He started when a tart and sensual intonation washed over him, sending desire crashing through him. It took a moment before what she wanted to know registered. The furniture—she wanted to know if he'd rearranged the room.

"Yeah, I did." Shifting forward in his seat, he waited for her to move closer, but she didn't. "You're quite observant, Ms. Navarro—most wouldn't have realized I'd moved the chair."

With the dim light streaming behind her, he thought he might have caught a shadow of the smile gracing her full lips as she turned but it was so brief he couldn't be sure. He bet she had a beautiful smile. Too bad he wouldn't ever see it.

"Funny, you're the second person this evening to mention it. But yes, I'm more observant than most. Now, if you'd be so kind to tell me how far I am from the bed, we can start this business."

Surprise washed over him. *She's that easy? No small talk, just show me the bed and let's get at it?* His libido purred at the idea, even as his conscience screamed at him to slow down. "It's in front of you."

"I'm well aware it's somewhere in front of me, Mr. Ra—"

"Nate," he interrupted. "If we're going to do this, I insist you call me Nate."

A heavy sigh escaped her. "Of course—we wouldn't want this to be too impersonal." She kicked off her shoes. "You're Nate and you can call me Xaviera if you wish." Reaching up, she freed her hair from the clip holding it off her neck. His fingers tightened around the arms of the chair. In the meager light, its thick, dark waves shimmered with red and bronze highlights as it spilled over her shoulders. He could envision fisting the strands as she gave him head. A harsh expletive passed his lips before he could stop it.

"Now why don't you tell me in specific terms where the bed is, so I can be comfortable as we talk?"

God, she's playing this fantasy to the hilt. I don't know if I should be offended or grateful. It took all his control to keep his response even-toned. "Ten feet ahead and three feet to the left." He watched as she walked forward, blocking the light before slipping into the shadows. A sigh of relief hissed past his parted lips when the springs on the bed squeaked. *One step closer to ending my self-imposed celibacy.*

"So, Nate, I think it's pointless to make small talk about who we are and what our jobs are, considering we both know why we're here." Her briskness stroked him the wrong way. He had to give her kudos for being honest though. They both knew they had contacted 1Night Stand to have a night of anonymous sex before parting ways in the morning, but his pride wouldn't allow him to give in so easily.

"You're assuming you know what I want, Xaviera. What would you say if I told you I wanted to see you again?"

A low chuckle drifted his way. "I'd say you're full of shit. You want the fantasy of screwing an anonymous woman for a night. No, you're not looking for strings—you're looking for physical release without guilt, just as I am."

"Perhaps." He almost wished he could read the look on her face but she was still in the shadows. "Or maybe it has to do with the fact if I don't get laid, I won't have a job."

She was silent before a giggle escaped her. "Lord only knows what kind of job would require you to get laid on a regular basis. Either way, I'm happy you showed." Her tone became more serious as she changed the subject. "I have a few questions before we do this, though. I trust Madame Evangeline did the proper background checks, but I need to hear it from you before we go any further. Are you clean and did you bring protection? Because if not, this ends now."

He shifted a bit before standing. Treading on light feet to the bed, he hovered over her. "Lady, I've never been with a woman without protection, let alone had a venereal disease, and I'll be damned if I'd sleep with a woman I just met without insuring my own health."

Whatever he'd expected her response to be, it wasn't what he got.

"Good to know. Now, shall we get to it? I haven't felt a man's touch in two years and I'm finding myself rather anxious." Her plea became soft and coaxing. "Nor have I felt a lover's skin under mine. The only question is, will you be the one to break my dry spell?"

"Fuck yeah." All thoughts of going slow were consumed by the undisguised need in her words. Using the fact his vision was already used to the darkness, he pushed her back on the bed before covering her mouth with a needy kiss. Damp lips parted under the pressure before the moist tip of her tongue slipped past his teeth to duel with his. A low, satisfied grunt pushed out of his chest when her slender arms wrapped around his neck.

Using his strength to his advantage, he half dragged, half lifted her farther up on the bed. Under him, her peaked nipples budded through her dress to rub against the bare skin of his chest. He was grateful he'd shed most of his clothes before she'd arrived. When she was where he wanted, he sank down over her, his hips parting her thighs.

The cool cotton of her dress brushed his sides. Gathering a handful, he hauled it up, loving the feel of her skin against him. Mindless with desire, he rocked against the cradle of her thighs, wanting nothing more than to sink into the hot, wet depths pressing against his stomach. *Son of a bitch she's so wet I can feel it through her panties.* Lifting his head, he drew a ragged breath, trying to slow down before he lost total control. "Damn, woman—you're like fucking dynamite."

Her fingers dug at his shoulders while she tried to pull him closer. "More! Don't stop." Her desperate plea made his nuts tighten.

"Not a prayer in hell. The hotel could be on fire and it wouldn't stop me." He reached out to trace a finger over the scalloped edge of her dress, teasing the rounded swells of her breasts. He couldn't see them clearly, but he needed the offending cloth gone. "How does this come off, sugar?" Not waiting for her to answer, he slid his hand under her, searching for buttons, a zipper, hell, anything that would tell him how to get the dress out of his way.

"Over my head." She breathed the words into his ear. Her tongue darted inside before abandoning the interior to nip at the lobe. "Sit up for a second."

He growled. The last thing he wanted to do was let go of the warm, sexy body under him. "Don't wanna." Licking her collarbone, he ground his erection against her mound.

"Only for a minute." She whimpered when he captured the tight nub of her breast, cloth and all between his teeth. He'd never heard anything sexier in his life. The urge to get inside her—to ride her, had him in its grip. His aching cock didn't care about slow and steady, it wanted fast and furious.

Her fingers dug into his hair when he switched breasts. Yanking one of the straps down far enough to loosen the top, he nosed aside the fabric as if in search of hidden treasure. Licking and nipping at every millimeter of skin he exposed, he grew close to finding it when she yanked hard on his hair. "Stop! Let me up, you teasing ass." Her breathing sounded harsh to his ears.

His lust-dazed mind tried to make sense of her words.

"Now? You wanna stop, now?" He yanked hard on the reins of his control, not so far gone he'd force an unwilling woman. His daddy had beat it into his head. It didn't matter if he had the head of his dick in a woman; if she said stop, you rolled off her and found the nearest body of cold water. No meant no. "Fuck!" Rolling away, he stood up, his body screaming in protest. The need that had been riding him earlier was minimal compared to the inferno inside him. Locking his hands behind his neck, he took deep breaths to calm himself while ignoring the rustling sounds behind him.

"Nate?" She touched his lower back.

He trembled as if a lash, rather than her soft hand, had touched him. His control was almost gone, making his tone gruff. "Yeah?"

"Get your ass back over here and finish what you started." Her finger curled around one of the loops on his shorts. "And don't forget the damned condoms because I'll kill someone if you stop again."

Chapter Three

Xaviera couldn't believe her own boldness. Even with her ex, she'd never been this demanding. Listening to him fumble with something, a drawer maybe, sent her desire higher. He would be her first lover since her accident, since she'd lost her sight, and she was nervous. *Perhaps that's why I'm pushing so hard. I'm afraid he'll stop. Thank God for the fantasy.*

A low gasp of relief fell from her lips as the bed dipped again. He was back. She cried out as he rolled over her, pinned both her hands next to her head as he straddled her. The hair-dusted thighs pressed against her sides tickled. He must've lost his shorts while he was grabbing the condoms.

"Sugar, are you trying to drive me nuts?" His hand cupped her left breast, his thumb teasing its nub. "Damn, you're naked. I wish I could see...." He sounded hoarse, his body moving against hers.

Panic flared. *Not now! I'm gonna die if he stops now.* "Remember the fantasy. You wanted the mystery...."

His groan whispered over her ear. "Shit.... How do you feel about giving head?" His stark need sent hers soaring. Her lips parted, her breathing grew ragged. The idea of feeling him against her tongue, filling her mouth with his hard flesh teased her. As much as she wanted it, the moment she got her mouth around his cock, she wouldn't be able to resist. Her fingers would find her aching clit and she'd come, and for once she didn't want to climax by her own hand.

"That depends." His uneven breathing told her how hot he was, but she wanted him to burn even hotter. "How do you feel about eating pussy?"

"Son of a bitch." His grip on her wrists tightened. "I love it. I can guarantee my mouth will find its way between your thighs tonight." His weight lifted off her. Expecting to feel the head of his dick brush her lips, she panted. "How about now? Eat me while I suck on your cock?"

She heard his sharp hiss. "Damn woman. I want this to last and sure as rain hits the ground, I'll come if I taste you while you have that sexy mouth wrapped around me."

Feeling his thighs tremble against her ribs, she imagined him poised over her, fighting his need. "And I'm going to come once I get you in my mouth. Don't let it be by my own touch." She arched off the bed, rubbing her stomach against his ass. "I need to feel a man—no, I need to feel *you* make me come. It's been so long." She no longer cared if it sounded like she was begging because she was. "Who said this had to be a one shot deal? Let's take the edge off, so we can enjoy a slow fuck."

His mouth pressed against hers, his tongue shooting inside to tangle with hers as he kissed her within an inch of her life. When he broke the kiss, she gasped for air.

"You are a dream come true, sugar." He released her wrists. With an economy of movement, his weight lifted before resettling on her. The brush of his silky length against her cheek had her head turning.

Wrapping a hand around him, she explored his dimensions as he parted her thighs.

"Ah loving hell, you're bare." She opened her mouth to ask if it was a problem, when his mouth closed over her and his tongue speared deep. *Evidently not.* As his lips, teeth, and tongue sucked, nipped, and licked, she was never more grateful that she'd continued her monthly trips to the spa. They had kept her soft and bare.

"Nate!" She squirmed under his relentless assault as he withdrew from her, only to lap at the crease of her thigh. Her fingers tightened around his length and jerked down, stroking the hard flesh, amazed when she couldn't quite encircle him. *Oh God, he's thick. Just the way I like them.* Squeezing hard, she wondered at the feel of holding a cock again.

"Please, suck me." His plea was whispered against the pulse in her inner thigh.

"Oh, yeah." Lifting her head, she used her hand to guide him to her lips. Latching onto the thick, bulbous head, she sucked, lapping at the dampness leaking from it. His hips surged, surprising her. She choked a bit as he slid deep into her mouth then brushed the back of her throat. Pushing helplessly at him, her eyes watered while she struggled to breathe. Panic surged before he withdrew.

"Sorry, sugar." His breathing was ragged. "Maybe this wasn't such a good idea."

Licking her lips, she savored the salty flavor of him. "Nonsense! Roll over. Let's try it with me on top."

He rolled with her and she thought she'd heard a muttered *Thank God* before she crawled over his muscled body. *God he's so firm. He's no desk jockey.*

She mewed like a kitten with pleasure.

Bringing her ass down to his face, smelling her desire, Nate groaned with relief as her mouth settled over his hard-as-nails dick. For a second there he'd thought he'd ruined it when he'd heard her choking noises and felt her hands pushing against him. Her mouth had felt so damn good, he'd reacted without thought, wanting nothing more than the wet heat she was offering. He'd expected her to either storm out of the room, or at least stop the oral sex in favor of fucking. While his body was glad she hadn't, he would've understood. No woman liked it when a man tried to force his cock down her throat. He hadn't expected her request for a change of position.

Her squirming and muffled gasps tickled every inch of his flesh. Cupping her hips, he angled his head up, determined to drive her insane with his mouth. Licking over the outer curve of her labia, he delved inside, searching for her taste. Tart, she exploded over his taste buds like grapefruit. She bucked toward his mouth, trying to get closer he assumed. When it caused him to lose his treat, he playfully smacked her hip. "Mine." She stilled at the sting and moaned around him. *God damn I hit the jackpot! Not only does she give head...*his breath stuttered as she tongued the sensitive underside of his cock...*but she doesn't seem to mind if I get a bit rough.* Pleasure sizzled along his shaft to settle at the base of his cock.

Wanting to give her the same bliss, he parted her folds, exposing the hard, little kernel of her clit to his gaze. "So damn hot," he gasped as her mouth slid down his length. Using his fingers to hold her open, he lashed at the swollen bud, loving her muffled shrieks as he coaxed her closer to rapture. Slipping two of his fingers inside her sheath, he growled when she reared back and her inner muscles milked them. "That's it, sugar. Ride 'em."

"Shit." Her moan reached him, then her hips rocked. Dipping his tongue to flick at the flesh surrounding his fingers, he savored her taste, giving a buck of his own hips when she tried to swallow him whole, sending him teetering on the edge. It had been too long since he'd felt a woman's mouth.

"Xaviera...sugar...you're gonna..." His balls drew up tight. "...I'm gonna come...please...." his words sounded like gibberish to his own ears. Struggling to hang on long enough to make sure she was with him was torture. Rubbing his thumb over her clit, he began finger-fucking her, hoping the brutal motion would send her over.

Her moans grew louder, until he hoped—no, he prayed she was there because he was coming whether she was ready or not. "Fuck...I'm coming...." Expecting her to lift her head to finish him off with her hand, he shouted when she tightened her lips around him. She sucked harder and brushed her fingers over a spot behind his nuts so sensitive he heaved under her slight weight, his cock unloading into her warm mouth. He locked in place as she continued to draw on him, until he sank back into the bedding, finally spent.

"Nate...please...." Her plea stroked over his over-stimulated flesh as she continued to rock against his palm, seeking her release. "...so close...I...." She buried her face against his thigh, her nails digging.

"Oh, sugar...." Rolling onto his side with her, he kept fingering her before sucking the swollen nub into his mouth. Tapping his tongue against it, he wanted to howl his pleasure when her tissues grabbed his fingers before releasing and grabbing again as she came for him. Yanking his hand away, he cupped her hips and rode out her orgasm, loving every scream, cry, and whimper she gave.

When she finally quieted, he let go of her clit and dragged his tongue down through her folds. Lapping at the juices trickling from her, he chuckled low when she jerked, trying to avoid his mouth.

"Enough...oh God...please...." Her pleas told him how thoroughly he'd pleasured her. Giving one last lick, he sank back, freeing her hips from his grasp.

Sprawled on his back, he stared up at the dark ceiling. He'd never felt so alive in his life. *Amazing what good sex will do for your outlook on life.* Sitting up slowly, he felt around for Xaviera. His hand encountered a shapely thigh. Smoothing his palm up and over her rounded hip, he couldn't resist giving it a generous squeeze.

"You okay, sugar?"

"Mmm-hmmm." The bed shook a bit as she sat up. "Just thirsty."

"Water, juice, or soda?" He rolled off the bed, reciting the contents of the en suite fridge. "Or something a bit harder?"

"Hmmm, orange juice sounds good."

From the rustling noise behind him, he assumed she had settled herself at the head of the bed. Gingerly picking his way toward where he thought the mini-fridge was, he cursed when his hip bumped into the corner of the table.

"Are you okay?" Her question floated over from the bed as he found the small fridge. He winced as the light from inside it made him see spots.

"Yeah." Snatching a couple of individually

wrapped boxes of juice, he straightened and closed the door. "Is from the carton okay?"

"Sure."

Moving back toward the bed, he managed to avoid the table but found the leg of the bedside stand instead. "Son of a bitch." His toes started to throb. He sank onto bed, cradling his foot. *Maybe I should've thought through this in-the-dark fantasy a bit better.*

"Oh for heaven's sake, Nate." The snick of the switch was his only warning as the room flooded with light.

Chapter Four

As soon as she flipped the light on, Nate blinked in surprise. Waiting for his eyes to adjust took several moments. Once he was able to see again, he stared down at the most drop-dead gorgeous, naked woman he'd ever laid eyes on. Lying back against the mound of pillows and rumpled comforter—hell, they hadn't even gotten around to turning the bed down—she lounged against the headboard with one arm thrown over her eyes as if to protect them from the light. She looked familiar, but he wasn't certain where he'd seen her.

A low growl built in his throat at the signs of their interlude. Her skin was still flushed from the orgasms he'd given her. The raspberry tips of her nipples which had been hard against his chest were soft and relaxed. They peeked out from under her long, dark hair. He could see the whisker burn from his stubble not only across the swells of her breasts, but on the insides of her creamy thighs. And heaven above, her bare mound tempted him beyond reason. She was absolutely exquisite. *Dear Lord, how did I get so lucky*? The idea she'd given him her body without inhibition had his cock stirring. He wished he could make love to her with the lights on. As tempting as it was, he couldn't. *I'd love to watch her every reaction.* He sighed. *It would be like a dream come true, until she caught a glimpse of my scars.*

The thought sobered him.

"I thought we agreed, there'd be no lights?"

"You demanded and Madame Evangeline agreed." Her tone was sleepy. "It really doesn't make a bit of difference to me, lights off or on, I'm still—"

Disbelief and anger coursed through him, killing his erection. The idea she didn't care enough to honor her end of the deal set him on edge. "What do you mean it doesn't matter? When I consented to meet you, it was under the promise certain provisions would be followed. I can't believe I fell for it. Just my luck, even on a blind date, I hook up with a bitch." When her arm dropped away from her face, he reached up and clicked the lamp off.

The bed rocked as she moved toward the opposite side. "I am not a bitch, Mr. Ramirez-Santiago. I accepted your terms, even though I didn't understand why a sighted man would want to fumble around in the dark."

Hearing the swish of what he assumed was her dress, his anger grew. *How dare she leave in the middle of our argument.* "Did you ever think that maybe it's because he doesn't want to watch his lover's eyes fill with pity?" When she didn't respond, his irritation grew. "Where the hell are you going?" He rose from the bed, surprised by the click of her shoes on the linoleum by the door. How had she gotten that far? He couldn't see a damn thing. His mind throbbed with confusion. Even pissed, he didn't want her to leave. *It's not like she saw anything. Maybe....* He groaned at the sound of the handle being turned. How the hell had he fucked this up? He couldn't—no, he refused to let her go. *I haven't had my fill yet. She can't leave me like this!*

Taking two steps, he tripped over his forgotten

shoes. Pain seared his forehead as his head struck the leg of what he thought might be a chair, before his body hit the floor. *What the fuck possessed me to move the damn chair*? Sitting up, he touched his forehead, his fingers coming away wet with blood. "Fuck, now I have nothing but my own stupidity to blame for adding another scar!"

There was a pause as the door was pulled opened. The light spilled into the room and around Xaviera, outlining her body standing just inside the threshold. Her shoulders slumped. She sighed, before her silhouette turned once more in the shadows. "Jesus Christ, you're worse at this than I was."

"The least you could do is check how bad I'm hurt before you leave. I think I tried to give myself a concussion and I'm bleeding. " Lame words, but he was desperate. "Besides, I'd like to know how the hell you managed to walk across the room earlier without killing yourself, when it's all I can do to make it five feet from the bed."

She moved with ease, running her fingers over the wall. It took her only a moment to find the switch. The room flooded with light, making him squint again. His eyes weren't taking kindly to the off and then on again scenario. When he finally opened them again, he saw her walk to the end of the bed before she stared off to his left.

"Lots and lots of practice." Shifting, a bitter laugh escaped her. "Unbelievable. Madame Evangeline sets me up with a man who wants everything done under the cover of darkness but doesn't even realize I'm blind. We should've been a match made in heaven. She apparently didn't factor in my rotten luck with men." Settling onto the edge of the bed, she motioned for him to come closer.

"Pardon the pun, but come over here so I can see how bad it is."

His brain befuddled, he couldn't help but stare at her in shock. "You're blind?"

A tug of her lips was all the emotion she gave away as she continued to stare into space. *Well not actually stare into space, you idiot. She can't see anything.*

"Yes, for the past eighteen months, sixteen days and thirteen odd hours. Since the morning I opened the hood of my car and changed my life forever." She patted the mattress next to her. "Come on, I don't have all night, Nate. I need to check on Lucy."

Surprise rolled through him, along with dread, but he didn't move. "Please tell me you don't have a kid waiting on you."

She shook her head. "No, no kids—just my dog." A brief smile touched her lips. "My faithful companion and the best trained seeing-eye dog around. She's waiting in my room."

It took a few painful and slow movements, but he was able to untangle himself from under the chair. He sank down on his knees. "Directly in front of you."

Her head cocked. "Are you now?"

He bobbed his head then cursed at himself for forgetting she couldn't see it.

A small laugh spilled from her. "You just nodded, didn't you?"

"Yeah."

Holding her hands out, she waited. He stared at her outstretched fingers. "What exactly are you doing?"

An exasperated sigh passed her lips. "Unless you want me to poke you in the eye, please guide my hands to where you injured your head."

Xaviera waited patiently, wondering what he would do. Would he accept the olive branch she offered? Or throw it back in her face? After a few agonizing moments, his warm hands settled on the back of hers. Allowing him to guide her, she bit her lower lip as her fingertips brushed over a bit of raised skin on his neck—a scar perhaps? *Maybe that's what he didn't want me to see.* Her attention wavered from the mystery of his motives as he guided her palm to his stubble-covered cheek before leading it up past his coarse textured eyebrows to a ragged patch on his forehead. Using a light touch, she traced the edges to determine the size.

"It doesn't feel too bad. I think you'll live." She stilled, her breath catching. "Ah, can I...?"

His breath teased her face. He was closer than she'd realized. "Can you what, sugar?" The raspy tone sent tingles of need to her womb. The release he'd given her earlier wasn't enough. She wanted more, but before that, she needed to know what his face felt like. She had to see him in her own way. But would he let her?

"Can I touch your face?" She nibbled on the inner curve of her lower lip, praying he would allow her to trace his features. "I know you don't want me seeing you, but it'd be nice to have an idea what you look like."

The rasp of his skin against her palm had her breath catching. He must've tipped his head against her hand. "Be gentle." The hesitant words were all she needed. Exploring, her fingertips brushed over high cheekbones, a nose that had been broken in the past if the lump in the middle was any indication.

Then slid down to drift over the full lips he'd pressed against hers earlier. Her tongue darted across her lower lip, remembering the way they'd felt.

"Sugar?"

Her heart leapt at the need-filled endearment. "Yeah?" She tried to ignore the tremble of her own voice. Desire wrapped around her once again. This time she had to feel him inside her, or go crazy.

"Will you tell me what happened?"

She stiffened as if she'd been doused in cold water. Having him ask her about how she'd lost her sight was the last thing she'd expected. *Especially when all I want is to climb back into bed with him.* Her sudden change of heart about leaving him to suffer alone in the dark should've surprised her but it didn't. Despite everything, his allowing her to touch his face when it was obvious he'd never intended for her to set eyes on him, had shown her a different part of his personality. The man possessed a soft side, even if he hid it behind a gruff exterior—one she wanted more than anything to explore.

"You don't have to tell me if you don't want to."

She sighed. "Do you really want to know? It's not a pretty tale."

"Neither is mine." He sounded rueful. "I'll tell you mine, if you tell me yours. I'd really like to know how you went blind. You inferred that you lost your sight because of something that happened with your car. Were you in an accident?"

Leaning back, she wished more than anything that she could see him. Being blind was a bitch. Most people didn't realize how hard it was to judge a person's reaction without sight. But as his hands rubbed slow circles on the tops of her thighs, it gave her the courage to relive the lowest point in her life.

"I was making a trip back home to the Napa Valley to visit my parents when I heard this clunking under the hood." She toyed with a loose piece of hair, an old nervous habit. "My dad always told me not to drive a car if it's making weird noises. I waited until traffic passed to lift the hood. It is the last thing I remember seeing."

"The radiator?" The softness of his reply gave away his concern while he continued stroking her.

"No. From what my father's mechanic said, the compressor was making the racket I heard. It was getting ready to let go. It was just my bad luck that I opened the hood as one of the air-conditioning hoses blew off—a high pressure hose he called it. Anyway, I got a face full of Freon. The next thing I remember was being found by a nice man and his wife. They were on a trip to Tahoe—that's where I run my family's small ski lodge—when they saw me lying on the side of the road, but by then it was too late. The chemical had damaged my eyes beyond repair." She stopped toying with her hair, deciding to take a chance he wouldn't overreact when he found out who she was. "I'm not sure how long I was there before they found me. But the result was quite obvious. Xaviera Navarro, the heiress to Navarro Wines, was blind and her fiancé of two years abandoned her just days before their wedding—because he couldn't deal with the pressure of being married to a blind woman." She forced a cheerful tone.

His thumb rubbed over her cheek. "He's an ass. If what you showed me is any indication of your talents, of how much you have to give, he's a gold-plated fool for letting you go. You're a very sensual woman, and any man would give his eyeteeth to have you under him."

For the first time in a long while, the melancholy which had become her life at Ryan's defection eased. It was hard to believe this man, a complete stranger, was soothing wounds she'd buried deep. So deep, at times she'd thought they'd never heal. She nuzzled his palm. More than anything, she wanted to give him a gift in return. Closing her eyes, she took the plunge. "I want you to make love to me, Nate." She held his hand to her face, hoping he understood she wasn't expecting to start a relationship, but that she didn't want to be alone tonight. "Just for one night, let me pretend a man can still physically love me— that I'm not totally useless."

Chapter Five

Nate's breath caught in his throat. Whoever said the eyes were the windows to the soul was correct. Even knowing Xaviera couldn't see him, the need for another's touch shimmered in the emerald depths of her eyes. She'd gone to 1Night Stand for the same reasons he had. To forget everything in favor of physical release—to leave their demons at the door and simply enjoy the feel of another's body against theirs in the dark.

"Oh, sugar." He cupped her check before trailing his fingers down her neck and across her collarbone. "I'd love nothing more than to lay you back on this bed, but it has to be more than just pretend. Our time together, while it lasts, will be real." His hand brushed over the swell of her breast to find her nipple. Toying with it through the cotton, he teased the nub until it strained against the material. A low moan vibrated against his shoulder where her face hid. "Nothing will be taboo and I'll claim every inch of you." Pressing his mouth against her ear, he nuzzled before tasting her skin. "Can you handle that, Xaviera? Belonging to me?"

"God, yes." Her admission released something primeval inside him. All he wanted was to claim her—to mark her in a way she'd never forget.

"Lie back," he whispered. "I want to explore." His hunger peaked as she obeyed with the slow lowering of her upper body to the bed. When she was positioned with her back and hips on the mattress, he lifted one slender leg until her foot was inches from his lips. Nuzzling her toes, he savored the giggle which escaped her before dragging his lips over her ankle. Tracking up her calf, he continued until he reached her knee and the lower edge of her bunched up skirt. Trapped by her legs, the skirt prevented him from going farther. "Lift." He nipped her inner thigh just above her knee when she was slow to respond. "You heard me, sugar. I can't reach your goodies and unless you want this pretty dress ripped...."

"Wild man, are you?" She wiggled, trying to free her foot.

He grinned. "You have no idea." Draping her legs over one shoulder, he hoisted her up, tired of her delay. With rough hands, he pushed the gauzy material above her waist; exposing the fact she hadn't put her panties back on—if she'd been wearing any to begin with. A low growl burst free at the idea of his lover being brave enough to walk around panty-less in a dress.

"Nate?" Lust and uncertainty radiated off her.

"Yeah?" Moving one leg to his other shoulder, he ran both hands down her thighs until they met at the juncture. Both of them moaned as his knuckles brushed over her bare mound. "So soft." Parting her folds, he stared at the glistening pink flesh. As succulent as a fresh Georgia peach. Tracing her opening, he pressed inside a bit with two fingers. The ring of muscles tugged at them, even as she cried out in pleasure. It caused his cock to throb. "So responsive." He kissed the inside of her knee as he forged deeper, loving the feel of her tightening muscles. It didn't take much imagination on his part to know what it would feel like around his cock. God he had to get inside her—now.

Pulling free of her warmth, he tried hanging onto his fraying control, even as he fumbled with a condom sitting on the edge of the bed. *Damn, it must've gotten tossed there during our wild sixty-nine.* "God, you're so tight. I can't wait." Ripping the package open with his teeth, he smoothed the thin prophylactic down his straining length. "Is missionary okay?" He'd promised nothing would be taboo but he found he couldn't wait. He should be worshiping her, exploring her pretty little breasts, licking and sucking their tight peaks, but his body was primed. He was on edge and needed inside her sweet pussy. "I'll be more inventive next time." He positioned the head of his cock against her, teasing them both.

A wavering smile crossed her face as she arched toward him trying to help. "Missionary is perfect. Just fuck me."

A low groan escaped him as he flexed his hips. With one quick snap, he was enveloped in living breathing fire. Electricity shot up his spine, and it was all he could do to keep from spilling right then and there. "Tight." He clenched his teeth, his fingers digging into her hips. It'd been too long since he'd felt the welcoming warmth of a woman's flesh.

"Please!" She writhed against him, trying to get him to *move.*

He stared down at their joining, noticing how her body had swallowed his. The sight of her creamy flesh against his own darker, much rougher skin, made him want to howl and beat his chest like a caveman. He'd claimed her and it went straight to his head. "Gimme a second, sugar, or I'm gonna be a thirty second wonder." Sweat dripped down the side of his face.

"Nate, please!" She trembled in his arms.

"I will." He tilted her hips a bit to sink deeper, watching as her chest wobbled under the bodice of her dress. "I want to gaze at your breasts. Show me."

Her chest heaving, a flush creeping up her neck, she obeyed. She slid her fingers under the straps resting on her shoulders, pushing them down. It took only a few twists and she was gloriously bare, with the soft fabric wadded up around her waist. A hoarse sound of need caught in his chest. "Tease them, sugar. I want to see your hands against them." He withdrew a bit, and pushed back in, unable to help himself when she did as he asked.

"Tell me what you see, Nate...please?" Hearing her uneven breathing and the quivering of her legs against his shoulders had him realizing how close she was.

He stilled. "Perfection, Xaviera. I behold two beautiful breasts tipped with hard, berry nipples I want to taste. I see a woman so lost to passion that she's abandoning herself to the pleasure of her own touch. I watch as fingers tug and pull, in just the right rhythm to cause the pussy holding me to contract around me...." He paused groaning when she clenched around him again. "Just like that." His head tipped back as his control snapped. "I'm sorry. I have to...." He thrust hard against her. "Tell me if I get too rough." His plea was lost as he was consumed by desire. Scrambling off his knees, he leaned over the bed, her legs still over his shoulders. Pinning her to the bed with his weight, he braced himself on out-stretched arms as his hips began to move.

"Oh my God, Nate!" Xaviera's fingers abandoned her nipples to dig into the bedding next to her hips. He was *so* thick. Doubled over as she was, she felt every inch of him as he bottomed out inside her. Climax beckoned and she fought to keep from going over. She wanted this to last.

"Fuck yeah." He moved against her. His chest heaved against the back of her legs. "Deep." He panted. "Need deeper." She squealed at the sharp pleasure buffeting her as he pressed her thighs to her breasts. He groaned and stopped. "Am I hurting you?"

She shook her head. "Don't stop! Oh God, don't stop." She squirmed as she stalled just below the peak. She whimpered in frustration. *So close—aw God I'm gonna die.* Reaching up to where she thought his face was, she brushed the nape of his neck. Tugging him down, she pressed her mouth to his. "Fuck me." The words were followed by a sharp nip to his lower lip. "Or I'm gonna hurt you."

"You asked for it." Pinning her hands to the bed, his hips started a fast, pummeling rhythm that had her sliding across the bed. Not that she cared. Lost to the world of sensations wracking her, she could've cared less if he knocked them onto the floor as long as he continued to fuck her. The room rang with his harsh breathing and her own mewing noises as the pressure mounted. She was right there. Just a few more thrusts and she'd go over.

She cried out when he jerked out of her. "Nate!" Her protest died when he flipped her over and sank into her from behind. Feeling him cover her, she nearly screamed when his fingers found her nipples and tugged before cupping her breasts.

"Hell yeah, better." His words tickled her ear. "I can play with these little beauties now." He groaned. "I love what it does to your pussy when I do." He gave her shoulder a teasing bite as one hand drifted down her stomach to toy with her clit. His thumb rubbed that special spot which sent her soaring. She screamed his name as she came apart under him. Bucking, she moaned into the bedding under her cheek, as both hands moved to settle on her waist. She hissed as he used his hold to jerk her back hard against him as his body tensed with his own release.

"Fuck!" His fingers had a nearly bruising grip as his hips continued to slap against her ass, forcing her own orgasm to double back and hit her again.

"Nate!" She writhed beneath him, trying to escape the too-intense pleasure he forced upon her body.

"Hell yeah—come again for me." He remained hard, continuing to thrust.

"Again?" Euphoria beckoned as another orgasm drew close.

"Yeah—once won't be nearly enough to sate me, sugar. Prepare yourself for one helluva a night." It sounded as if he spoke through gritted teeth. This was one of the few times she didn't have to be able to see to hear the promise or the sensual threat in his voice. She was too busy falling over the edge again.

***

Several hours later, Lucy—retrieved from down the hall—was on the floor beside the bed, Xaviera snuggled closer to Nate. Propped against the headboard of the bed in a sea of pillows, she accepted the strawberry from his fingers. After they'd called the desk, she'd finally remembered the cart Jackson had left for them. Now they were talking about nonsense things as he fed her and they sipped at glasses of wine from a still slightly-chilled bottle of her family's finest Chenin-Blanc.

"I can't believe Jackson bothered with finding a bottle of this." She licked the rim of her glass. "I'll admit it's a stroke of genius on his part. If he treats all his guests this way, it's easy to understand why his family's hotels and resorts are so popular."

"Hmmm," Nate's nose nudged the side of her neck. She giggled when his tongue laved the pulse there.

"Nate!" She tried to push him away. It seemed as if he was ready for another round of loving. She'd never had a lover as exuberant as him. He'd taken her three times already and it that still wasn't enough. While it thrilled her that he was so insatiable, she still hadn't heard his story—why he'd wanted the anonymity of darkness. "Knock it off, lover boy. Fess up." Tangling her fingers in his hair, she gave it a playful tug.

"Aw, sugar...don't be that way. We have much better—and less depressing things we could be doing...." She could just see the pouting little boy in his tone. He licked her pulse before raking his teeth over her collarbone.

She wiggled away and crossed her arms over her breasts. "No more nookie until you tell me why you wanted it to be in the dark."

He sighed before moving to settle next to her. She was surprised when he took her hand and placed upon his left wrist. "Fine, be that way...but I expect another one of those killer blow-jobs for this." As he teased her with his words, he pulled her hand up to the crook of his elbow. Under her fingers was roughened skin. Unlike the lower part of his arm which was covered with silky hair, it was devoid of hair. She recognized a scar when she felt it. A lump grew in her throat as she settled against his chest.

"I'll give you a couple of them," she promised solemnly.

"I'm a fire jumper by trade...you know what that is?" He guided her hand up his shoulder. *Still more scarring.* His reluctance started to make sense.

"Yes. You jump out of a perfectly good plane to fight forest fires."

His chest rumbled under her ear. "And on the rare occasion into a canyon where the shrubbery has caught on fire because of the drought and some careless kids with fireworks."

"So you jumped in and got burned?" She felt the movement of his head above her.

"Yeah. When I got into the canyon, I found a little boy surrounded by smoke and flames. Later they determined he was responsible for starting it. He was only eight and didn't mean to—all he had wanted to do was light some bottle rockets his mother had told him to wait until later to do." He paused and exhaled loudly. "I was in there trying to get this little boy to stop crying. He was scared, you see. I fell from the sky in full garb...helmet, breathing mask, and everything. I imagine that I looked like a monster to him. Each time I tried to get close, he'd smack at me. I ended up having to take off my mask and helmet to prove I wasn't a monster."

He shifted a bit under her as if mentally girding himself. "It was about that time a tree behind him fell toward us. Without thinking I reacted—I covered his body with mine. But without my helmet or mask, a

branch that was on fire landed on my exposed neck—
and somehow managed to slide down the inside of
my jacket." His hand pulled hers up past his
shoulder. "I ended up with second and third degree
burns....and like your fiancé, my girlfriend eventually
left. Of course, this wasn't until I tried to make love to
her the first time after the accident. She actually
jerked away from me, saying she couldn't sleep with a
man as horribly disfigured as I was. She tried, but she
just couldn't." Instead of sounding bitter, his tone
was more resigned. "So there's many reasons why I
didn't want you to see me. Pity and rejection being
the primary ones."

"Did you save the little boy?" She couldn't care
less about the idiot woman who'd tossed this man
away. The little boy's life was more important and she
wanted to remind him of that.

"Yeah. Although after he was treated for smoke
inhalation and returned to his hysterical mother, I'm
sure he probably wished I hadn't." He rubbed a hand
over her back. "She was ready to take a strip off him
for scaring her so badly."

A giggle escaped her before she cupped his chin.
Tipping her head back she stared at where she
thought his face was. "I assure you, your girlfriend is
worse than a gold plated fool, Nate. To have a man
like you as her own—one who puts himself on the line
for others and is an excellent lover—and throw him
away because of a few scars, is ridiculously stupid.
She didn't deserve you, but her loss is my gain."

She snuggled back down to rest her cheek
against his chest. The silence grew between them
until he finally spoke—his voice was rough. "So you
would've kept me?"

"Hell yes." She soothed her palm over his

shoulder. *I'd love to keep you—too bad this is only to be one night.*

"Then keep me." He rolled her over onto her back. "Don't let this end here, sugar." His knuckles brushed over her cheek as he tucked a piece of hair behind her ear.

Her breath caught. "But this was only supposed to be...."

He pressed a finger to her lips. "I know, but I want more of you—I'm not ready to walk away. We'll go slow—no strings, no pressure. I just want to get to know you—to see if this can go anywhere. Please give it—us a chance."

Nibbling on her lip, she tried to weigh her options. She was still scared but unless she tried she'd never know...and deep inside she trusted him. "Okay, we'll try."

He gave an excited yell, causing Lucy to stir next to the bed. She yipped and Xaviera laughed. "It looks like Lucy approves too."

He chuckled. "So, it would seem." His nose touched hers. "So...since you promised me a blow job, what would you say to another sixty-nine?"

Her breath caught in her throat and her nipples beaded at thought. "I'd say you're on."

The End

Wyk's Surrender

She wants to mark him and make him hers....

Mistress "V" lusts after her boss. She wants him at her mercy, begging for her touch, but he only knows her as his very capable assistant Venus. When an off-hand comment dashes her hopes, the sexy domme turns to Madame Eve at 1Night Stand for help....

He isn't sure he can handle the dark pleasure she promises....

Living up to his father's expectations has driven Wyk Havas to the edge. His curvaceous assistant Venus wants to push him past those limits, and he's damn near attracted enough to try. But Venus's preference for men to submit to her threw him for a loop. Can a date from 1Night Stand show him if he's able to submit to a woman?

Can Wyk truly surrender to Mistress V's pleasure or were they doomed from the start

Chapter One

"*P*lease, Mistress!" The naked man trembled at her feet, every inch of his creamy mocha skin glistening with sweat. His shoulders flexed and strained, as he tugged at the jute restraints at the base of his back. She loved the contrast of the off-white material and his dark arms. His head, shaved bare at her request, hung down with his chin on his chest. In between his splayed thighs, rose his cock, long and hard. A shiny trail of moisture on the thickly veined shaft tempted her to taste. Everything, from his submissive pose to his arousal and subsequent plea, sent a fresh jolt of desire down her spine.

Her submissive, the man who'd placed his trust in her, inhaled sharply when the flogger hit her leg with a loud crack. In the past, he'd begged to feel her favorite toy against his back, or any other part of him she chose. Tapping the flogger, she moved around him, drawing his attention with her studied movements. Dragging the strands over his shoulder as she circled him, she hid her smile. The mirrors showed her every moment, if he dared to peek. And he'd dare, if only to get caught.

"What do you want, slave?" With a flick of her wrist, she released him.

"Anything you'll give me, Mistress."

She frowned at the standard but routine reply.

She wouldn't accept generic from her submissive. He would reveal his secrets, his desires, and entrust them to her without reservation. She would settle for nothing less.

"That is not what I asked, slave." She continued to circle his kneeling form, coming to a stop in front of him.

"It's all I have to give, Mistress." His voice was rough as his chest rose and fell erratically.

Her hand went to her hip. A low hiss passed her lips. His frustration should be sexual and despite his obvious erection, she hadn't pushed him that far yet. Using the handle of the flogger, she lifted his chin to chastise him, to demand he give her the answers she wanted. The words died on the tip of her tongue as the dark honeyed eyes of Chadwyk "Wyk" Havas pinned her in place. The lust, anger, and desperation in her boss's gaze took her breath away, even as it stroked her need to dominate higher. Her empty sheath clenched hard, a trickle of cream escaped her, and her nipples hardened against her corset. Wyk would give her what she wanted. Here in her playroom he had no authority. She was the one in charge....

The strident blast of Venus Spinazzola-Navarro's alarm tore her from her torrid dream to start the day. She jerked upright in bed, the sun streaming through her window. Pushing the silk sheets away from her overheated body, she cradled her head. She fought for the hard won control she'd learned at Master Wong's side. *Nothing more than a dream.* Mr. Havas didn't belong to her. He didn't sleep at her side, nor would he ever. As his executive assistant, she would never mix business and pleasure, even if she thought the man willing. *Which he isn't.* When it came up during some after-work drinks, his vocal distain for the lifestyle had cut her to the core. So why was she *still* dreaming about the unattainable?

Perhaps she should contact Master Wong. Maybe he could give her some answers. She'd resisted the urge so far; her mentor would advise her not to pursue such a man. Plenty of other submissive males existed out there. And that she, an experienced Domme, could have her pick. She could crook her finger, and despite or perhaps because of her well-rounded figure, they would come running. She didn't have to settle for erotic dreams that left her damp with unsatisfied desire. But none of the men at the club appealed to her. None had even nudged her need to dominate.

"Which is why this has to work. That damned matchmaker better come through."

Naked as usual, she crossed her darkened bedroom to the ornate master bathroom. As a larger-than-average woman, she'd taken one look at the tiny bathing stall and called the plumber. It'd taken a couple weeks after she purchased the condo for them to install the spacious state-of-the-art walk-in shower but at times like these, she didn't regret the expense and time.

Opening the glass door, she stepped inside the huge tiled monstrosity and cranked on the water. Various nozzles came to life as her pre-programmed settings adjusted the temperature and pressure so when she stepped under the spray the water pounded over her body. It could almost peel her skin off. She sighed. *Just the way I like it.* She braced her hands against the slick wall in front of her and closed her eyes.

As the water massaged her body, she forced Wyk from her mind. Instead, she focused on her future blind date. The one Xaviera had talked her into. She'd almost backed out once she'd received the long questionnaire and background check she'd had to complete, but Xaviera wouldn't let her. Her cousin had harped and bullied her into going forward. She'd insisted this would be the perfect solution for her problem. And after meeting her relative's fiancé, a wonderful man Madame Evangeline had set her up with, she could only pray the matchmaker would have the same luck with her. It would take a miracle to find the perfect submissive man to exorcise Wyk Havas from her dreams, so she could move on with her life. But she had to get through a morning of work, face the object of her lust, and resist temptation before she could board the plane to Vegas for Xaviera's wedding that evening. It would be a long day.

***

Wyk Havas groaned, driving his fist up and down his length. The act shamed him, even as it sent dark, forbidden pleasure through him. Hard and swollen, his cock and groin were tight with need. Once again, he'd sought refuge in the small bathroom off his office. Masturbating at work because of his assistant had become a habit. The beautiful, frumpy, curvaceous Venus was his personal Botticelli. Her Rubenesque form caused his hands to itch with the need to touch, while his mouth hungered for her taste. He'd tried to resist. Denied his lust for weeks until the pressure became unbearable.

He'd first given in to the need for private release after coming upon her bent over one of the low filing cabinets. The move pulled her slacks tight across her voluptuous ass, outlining every curve. He'd emerged from his office to ask her about a missing form in a client's file. His mouth had gone dry, his cock hard, and he'd crushed the file in his hands before he'd realized what he was doing. If it hadn't been for another co-worker's arrival, he'd have sunk to his knees behind her and begged her to let him taste every inch of the rounded surface. The need had shaken him to the core and he'd escaped into the bathroom where he'd jerked off. After a half-dozen strokes, he'd sprayed the sink with his release. Afterward, he hadn't been able to look at himself in the mirror. He'd vowed it wouldn't happen again.

But it had been a promise he'd broken, over and over. At first, only every couple of weeks, but as he'd begun to peel away Venus's outer prickly layers, it became a weekly, then almost a daily occurrence. The inner strength under her conservative pantsuits and competent skills as his assistant turned him on faster than a stripper clad in pasties and a thong. Almost as much as the conversation he'd overheard.

He hadn't meant to eavesdrop when he'd tried to dial out to check on his reservations for his flight to Las Vegas, but he hadn't hung up when he heard her voice either. He'd damned near dropped the phone, when Venus said she planned to use her "date" in every way imaginable, until she drove some damned man out of her dreams. He'd eased the receiver back on to its cradle after she giggled and began to describe some of the things she planned to do to the unsuspecting man. Then he'd fled to the bathroom, tearing at his zipper until he'd freed his cock.

Palming his shaft, he groaned. How he wanted to be the lucky man to receive her attentions. To give her what she needed, to give up his control and let her do what she willed with his body. It didn't matter that his dad had always told him that as a proud black man he should never bow down to another. He wanted the forbidden. To have her order him around, demand he please her. His grip tightened as her stern voice warned him against coming, insisting he hold his release until she gave permission. His breath grew more ragged as his orgasm approached. His balls drew up tight. His arm trembled; his hips thrust. He was so close.

"Mr. Havas?" Venus's voice floated through the door. He gritted his teeth to keep from calling her to him. If she so much as touched the bathroom door, he'd fall to his knees and beg her to let him taste her, to love her.

"Damnit, where did that prick go to now? If he's left the office again without telling me, I'll take a single-tail to his ass, boss or not. How many times do I have to tell him I can do my job better if he'd simply let me know when he steps out?" Frustration filled her voice.

His assistant always wanted to know when he left the office or went to meetings. The dark promise in her tone, however, stroked over him, and he lost it. He bit down on his lower lip to keep from screaming and pulled hard on his dick. Lightning raced up his spine as his seed exploded over the white porcelain basin. He shook through his climax, every nerve alive with pleasure, until he sank to the floor, exhausted but exhilarated.

When the outer door to the office clicked shut, he clutched the edge of the sink and levered himself into an upright position. His rumpled reflection in the mirror stared back at him. He couldn't go on like this. Something had to give. He'd either fire Venus and hire a new assistant, or go on this damned 1Night Stand blind date thing and see if he could give over to a woman. He'd thought the idea absurd when Nate, a friend from back home, had told him how he'd met his blind heiress, but he was desperate. If this Madame Eve could set him up with a Domme, and he found he could let go, there was a chance—a slight one, he might be able to earn Venus's forgiveness along with a place in her life.

Washing his hands, Wyk made his choice. Fantasizing about his assistant telling him how to pleasure her, commanding his responses, even punishing him when he slipped, kept him up at night. Until, scared and sleep-deprived, he'd put his foot in his own mouth. He still regretted the evening Venus had mentioned how she enjoyed dominating men in her personal life, and he'd panicked and he'd chosen to degrade the very thing he wanted.

Hopefully this date will be a step in the right direction. Maybe it will prove how wrong I was when I ridiculed her choice of lifestyle.

Chapter Two

"I can't freakin' believe I'm doing this," Venus muttered as she shed the fussy chiffon dress she'd donned earlier in the evening as Xaviera's maid of honor. Out of sorts due to her struggle to ignore Wyk as he did his duty as Nate's best man, she was ready to jump out of her own skin. When she'd agreed to make the arrangements, she hadn't been aware of his role in the wedding. Nate had referred to him as Chad, a name foreign to her. To her, he'd always been the irresistible, got her panties wet Wyk. It had been a surprise to walk into the area they'd roped off for Xaviera's wedding and see him dressed in a midnight blue tux, as handsome in formal wear as in his slacks and polo shirts. His smirk had grated on her nerves.

Despite the tension between her and her boss, her cousin's wedding in front of a charming fountain was beautiful. Xaviera, a vision of loveliness in a lacy, cream-colored gown with modest train. Nate, her groom, had appeared ruggedly handsome in a classic black tuxedo despite the faint scars on his neck and jaw. But Lucy, Xaviera's seeing-eye dog, sitting between them with tendrils of baby's breath woven around her harness, had stolen the show. The beautiful black lab was one of the best-behaved dogs Venus ever had the pleasure of meeting. Lucy had even woofed when the minister had asked who gave the bride in marriage, causing a chuckle. Then, of course, came Nate and Xaviera's vows. They had been simple but poignant and the kiss so sweet, Venus's heart had nearly melted. Well, until the innocent peck had warped into something hotter, and she'd been tempted to push both of them into the fountain to cool them off.

Once the reception started and the bride and groom cut the cake, she'd slipped away, determined to put "you know who" from her mind. She would enjoy her date, even if it killed her. Wyk would probably find a fawning female who wouldn't mind letting his charm sweep her off her feet and into his bed. Plenty of available women wandered about the Castillo's flagship hotel. Instead of dwelling on his plans, she'd focus on get ready for *her* late night rendezvous with the man Madame Eve had picked for her.

Tossing the dress over the end of her still immaculately made bed, she paused by the array of items she'd placed out earlier in preparation. Sex wasn't promised, but if things went as she hoped, she would have a chance to use these on her very willing date. She trailed her fingers from the flogger to the silk sleep mask she planned to use as a blindfold, and let her mind wander to her plan of attack for the evening like every well-prepared Domme did.

The information packet Madame Eve had faxed to her at the hotel contained a wealth of information about her date. More than normal, if Venus were to guess, because of her particular requests. But it would give her a guideline of what the man wanted, so in turn he could give her what she needed. The possibility of training a man who longed to be submissive but had no real experience with the lifestyle stroked her libido higher, while it satisfied an emotional urge as well.

Was she asking for a stand-in for the man she wanted? Yep. But maybe the reality of dealing with a newbie would cure her of her craving to the point she wouldn't long to jump Wyk every time she saw him. The flogger, restraints, blindfold, and simple leather collar went into the small black bag already holding an adjustable cock ring, anal plug, and a never-opened box of condoms. As prepared as she could be, she took it out to the sitting room and returned to the bedroom.

Walking over to the small table in the corner, she skimmed the file's contents once more. Her date was a black man who worked in a position of power in his vanilla life, but requested anonymity for his foray into the BDSM world. He had stated a need for a strong woman, capable of taking charge; one who understood her needs and wasn't afraid of expressing them.

"Well, buddy, I hope you realize what you asked for. As desperate as I am, you may not be able to do anything other than moan when I'm through with you."

She tossed the sheaf of papers back on the table and squeezed the bridge of her nose to stave off her half-assed headache. At that moment, she just wanted to crawl into bed and snuggle up against a hard shoulder. Between her torrid dream this morning, the disappearing act her boss had pulled, the long flight from Chicago to Las Vegas, and the last minute madness for Xaviera's wedding, the soon-to-be migraine had crept up on her. Perhaps a hot shower and a light meal would put her to rights. She wouldn't waste this once in a lifetime chance to exorcise a certain man from her fantasies. After placing an order with room service, she headed toward the bathroom.

***

Wyk wiped his damp palm over his slightly bristled scalp. Directions from his date passed through his brain even as he listened to the voice on the other end of the cellphone. He had to shave again, and his toiletry bag lay buried somewhere in his suitcase. The spectacular lights of the Vegas strip shone through his parted curtains. Not that he could give it the attention it merited. He was too busy trying to distract his dad. The last thing he would tell his strict Catholic father was he didn't have time to talk because he had to get ready for a date. His dad would want to know particulars about the woman he couldn't even begin to tell the old man.

"I know, Dad." He tossed his unearthed toiletry bag on the bathroom counter. "Can't you get Seb to go with you? He loves cat fishing." Toeing his loafers off, he turned on the shower. A courier had dropped a packet with requested preparations. His date had laid out exacting conditions. She would participate as long he followed a few simple rules. He must be clean-shaven, including his head. The woman must have a thing for bald black men. *Which is a good thing.* The first time he'd done it, his college girlfriend had scratched at his scalp when he went down on her. The small bite of erotic pain had tripped his trigger.

His dad continued to gripe, finally asking Wyk if he was listening. He dragged his attention away from anything to do with sex to focus on placating his father.

"I know I promised to come down this weekend. I'm sorry I forgot to call, but I got busy at work and it slipped my mind. I didn't expect Nate to call me out of the blue a couple of weeks ago and ask me to stand up with him during his wedding. Even if I caught a flight back to Chicago tonight, I wouldn't be much use to you. Jet lag can be a real bitch. So I called to let you know I wouldn't be able to come tomorrow, before I head back down to the reception." Satisfied with the water temperature, he shut the shower door. "I'm not about to leave my buddy hanging." His dad understood loyalty. After a couple more minutes of good-natured grumbling, his dad agreed to call Seb before hanging up with an order to kiss the bride. Pressing the end button, he tossed his cell on the counter.

Flicking the small buttons on his dress shirt open, he rolled his head in an effort to ease some of the tension in his neck and shoulders, which had built up since the wedding. The event had gone off without a hitch. With Venus in control of the arrangements, no one had dared to mess up her cousin's special day. But it'd done a number on his libido to see her lush figure draped in champagne pink chiffon and her dark red hair in an elaborate up-do. Not to mention the shimmery hose that peeked out from the fluttering hem of her dress. He hadn't been able to stop thinking about how her long legs would feel draped over his shoulders as she ordered him to eat her pussy. The cool disdain in her eyes had done little to temper his ardor either. Just the sight of it had him wanting to drop to his knees and tell her to do what she willed with him.

He jerked the clasp on his tux pants open and

eased the zipper down, being careful to not catch himself in the teeth. Letting the pants pool at his feet, he wrapped his hand around his dick to comfort it. He had no idea if sex would be on the agenda tonight, but a man could hope. It'd been too long since he'd been laid. He needed this, even if the match Madame Eve had set him up with was nothing more than a stand-in. He'd shave his entire body if that's what it took.

He turned to the sink, as the bathroom filled with steam. The water needed to be hot or he'd stiffen up. Four years of playing college ball had left its mark on him. After the long flight out, the steamy shower would be a welcome relief. While he shaved his jaw, he thought about the questions Madame Eve had said the woman would ask before they proceeded. Some of them made him hard, while others made him feel raw, exposed. Could he do this? Could he lay his soul open to a woman he'd just met?

He wiped the moisture off the mirror. Then he lathered his scalp with shaving gel and scraped away the stubble with practiced motions while contemplating his decision. Yeah, he might be able to, given the right incentive. All he could do was pray the Domme knew how to handle an inexperienced submissive.

He would have to trust Madame Eve's judgment. And after witnessing the wedding downstairs, he had to give the woman kudos. If she could find that stubborn bastard, Nate, a perfect mate, she could do anything. By the time he finished shaving, the glass had fogged over again.

He pushed his way under the spray and hissed in pleasure. Reaching for his bottle of body soap, he lathered up, paying close attention to every nook and cranny. After his long day of travel, he didn't want to offend his date. Drawing a soapy washcloth over his balls and cock, he gave the flesh a squeeze and resisted the urge to rub one off. Mistress V, as she called herself, had forbidden any form of release while he got ready. So instead of a long jerk session, he would treat himself to the massage option on the shower head. Hopefully the pounding spray would help relax him before he met his date in the suite next door.

ChapterThree

Distracted from her steamy FemDom story by a sound in the next room, Venus cocked her head and set down her e-reader. Had her date already arrived? If it was Madame Eve's selection, the man was early, really early. She enjoyed punctuality as well as the next girl, but thirty minutes? She had specifically requested his presence at half-past the hour. If the man couldn't follow her orders, it would be a long night for both of them. Swinging her bare feet over the edge of the mattress, she continued to listen. When the sound came again, she lightly trod to the inner suite door she'd left ajar.

She gazed into the sitting room. Her date had arrived. Standing in the foyer, he kicked off his shoes and stripped off his T-shirt. Irritation flowed through her, despite the fine condition of his dark body in exercise shorts. His abs were well-defined, with a smattering of tight curls below his navel.

Her eyes strayed away from his washboard stomach as he struggled into the basic leash position she'd requested. Dropping to his knees, he parted his thighs. Her mouth went dry when the material of his shorts stretched tight over his upper legs and groin, cupping and accenting his cock and balls. She'd never seen a sexier sight, but when he gave a muffled grunt as he crossed his arms behind his back, she shook her head. The over-anxious fool would end up with a pulled muscle or something if he wasn't careful. She entered the room with a sigh, shutting the door behind her. The loud click had the man's head swinging up in her direction. Thankfully, she stood in the shadows cast by the lone lamp on the far side of the room, because nothing in her life as a Domme had prepared her for the reality of Wyk Havas kneeling before her, his body exposed to her gaze. Her heart raced. She backed up until she ran into the closed door.

This had to be a joke. Madame Eve couldn't have set her up with Wyk. There would be no way her boss would ever submit to someone like her. She fumbled with the door handle, in an effort to escape, but when he continued to kneel, not speaking, her nerves settled. Perhaps he did want this. Other than his early arrival, he had followed her instructions. Not to mention the key card he had to possess to enter her suite. Even though it looked like this man was her date, she still worried it was a sick joke on his part. More than once she'd cursed her loose tongue when she'd accepted his offer for after-work drinks. After a few too many glasses of red wine, she'd have spilled more than the mere fact she was a Domme if it hadn't been for the shocked look on Wyk's face. *And my boss never treated me the same again.*

"Mistress V?" Her name came out a bit hoarse, drawing her attention. His dark eyes shone with uncertain need as he fidgeted under her stare. A sigh escaped her when he used her Domme name. She could do this. He probably didn't have a clue he'd flown halfway across the country for a date with his assistant. Would he be angry when he found out? An idea formed in her head.

"Eyes down, slave." She injected enough steel

into her voice that his gaze lowered. "When was our set meeting time?"

"Eleven-thirty, Mistress." He started to lift his head, but stopped when she growled with displeasure.

"And what time is it now?" She moved toward the sideboard. Unzipping her bag, she pulled the satin sleep mask out, along with the flogger. With the items in hand, she approached him on light feet until she stood close enough to hear his shallow breathing. A low sound passed his lips. He sounded nervous. He had reason to be. A ticked-off Domme was never a good thing—at least not for the submissive.

"It was a few minutes past eleven when I left my room, Mistress." He shifted to look up at her.

"Eyes down, slave." She dropped the blindfold between his knees. "So you arrived a full thirty minutes ahead of time."

"Yes, Mistress. I was anxious."

"Why?" She glided to his left, circling him as she did in her dreams. His back was as tempting as his front, the well-defined layers of muscle trembling under his chocolate skin. She itched to place her mark on them. To cause his dark flesh to redden from her flogger, to dig her nails into his shoulders while she rode him, or to test them with her teeth. Would she be able to tell, or would his coloring hide the evidence of her claim on his body?

"I don't know, Mistress."

His evasive answer pricked her ire, and she flicked the flogger against her denim-covered thigh. He jumped at the sound. "If you're going to lie to me, this date is over. Honesty is one of the rules you agreed upon. Without it, your submission will be as flawed as my dominance. I refuse to fail because you lie to avoid the reason you came. Leave, if you can't give me the truth."

"Fine." He rolled his shoulders. "I saw a woman earlier. One who...I hope this date will prepare me for. I needed to get started on it, before I chickened out."

Hurt that he'd come to her for another threatened to overwhelm her, but she pushed the feelings back. "So this date is a dry run for the woman you want?"

He nodded.

"Words, slave."

"Yes, Mistress. I hope this will prepare me for what she needs," he whispered.

"And what about what you need, slave?" She studied the back of his bent head. He'd freshly shaved his scalp. It sent a thrill through her that he'd done so to please her. If she touched, would it be soft as a baby's bottom?

"I want this—I think." His uncertainty radiated off him. It excited her, but part of her, the more jaded part, insisted she walk away. She'd never taken an unwilling submissive, and she wouldn't start now.

She stroked the flogger over his bare shoulder, letting the leather strands brush his skin. His breath caught in his throat, and a shiver worked down him. Oh yes, he liked the play of leather against his skin, but she needed some assurance he could handle her desires. If he could, she'd use the blindfold and take what she needed. Screw what would happen at work on Monday. Perhaps, if she did it right, Wyk wouldn't even realize it had been her. But first she had to give him one last out, one more chance to call it off before things got serious. "You think you want this?"

He started to nod but uncertainly and frustration

flashed across his face "I want to serve. To submit to her. To have her tell me how to please her; to have her withhold my pleasure when I screw up."

Her nipples tightened against her tank top as her cream dampened the seam of her jeans shorts. "What if this woman yearns to teach you? What I enjoy with a submissive may not be what she enjoys. Each Domme is different. You could be wasting your time learning my preferences."

His shoulders sank. "It's more than that. I want to see if *I* can do this. If I can offer my submission to her. If it will fill up the empty spot inside of me."

She'd warned him. If he still insisted, she would take what he had to offer. "Fine, slave. I'll give you a choice. You have five minutes. In front of you there is a sleep mask which will double as your blindfold. If you decide you don't want to go through with this, simply leave. I'll contact Madame Eve and tell her we didn't mesh. Perhaps, she'll be able to find another better suited for you. However, if you wish to see where this leads, when I return I expect you to be wearing the mask and nothing else."

"But the letter said to wear exercise shorts, Mistress."

She smiled at his protest. "Just like the letter said you were to arrive at eleven-thirty, slave. Tit for tat. You broke one of the rules, so I am within my limits to change another." She moved toward the bedroom. "Five minutes, slave." Then she slipped into the bedroom, closed the door behind her, and leaned against it. Every part of her hummed with tension. *Dear Lord, please let him decide to stay.*

Wyk let out a ragged breath after the door shut behind Mistress V. She had to have recognized him.

He'd nearly died when he'd caught a glimpse of her lush form before she'd stepped back into the shadows. His heart pounded until he thought it might jump out of his chest. The moment was upon him. He had to make a choice because once she came back into the room, there would be no escape. He weighed his decision. He wanted what she had to offer, but what price would he have to pay for the experience? Because his executive assistant would be ruthless. He just wished he could figure out what Venus wanted. Should he take the risk and gamble on winning? Go along with her ruse, in hopes she wouldn't run in the harsh light of day? Or call her on her deception, before admitting how desperate he was?

He couldn't hide his desire for her. She wore a pair of jeans shorts and a royal blue tank top that molded to her curves. It'd taken all he'd been able to muster to drop his head and not reach for her. At first he'd thought they'd have a knock down-drag out battle over the irony of Madame Eve's choice, followed by her kicking him out of her room. But she hadn't. Instead she'd used the shadows to her advantage. She'd circled him, questioned him, even teased him with the flogger from the dark bag on the sideboard. It'd only stroked his need higher. What other goodies had she stashed inside it, and what she would do with them if he stayed?

He rubbed his hand over the back of his neck and stared down at the blindfold. In the end, he had to decide if the promise of more was worth the risk. She could very well walk away in the morning as if nothing happened. *If I let her.* He tried to weigh the pros and cons, but it didn't seem to matter in the end. He had chosen his path the moment he'd walked through the door of her suite. There would be no backing out. He'd deal with the fallout tomorrow. He wanted what Madame Eve had promised in her e-mail—a night to remember.

Rising to his feet, he hooked his thumbs in the waistband of the shorts. He shoved them down and kicked free of the silky material. The neat freak in him bothered by the idea of leaving them on the floor, he folded and set the shorts on the sideboard. Then he returned to his previous position. Kneeling with his legs parted, his dick exposed, he snagged the blindfold from the floor. It took less than thirty seconds for him to slip the simple mask over his head and position on his face. Now he waited for his prickly assistant to return.

Chapter Four

Cracking the door open, Venus resisted the urge to tuck her hair behind her ear. She would look at this as if Wyk were any other sub who wanted, no, needed her attention. If he stayed. He might have decided to leave. To find out, all she had to do was enter the sitting room.

She gathered her Domme persona around her on the chance he remained, then strode into the room. The sounds of her bare feet were muffled by the plush carpet. As she moved past the settee, she stumbled to a stop. In all his luscious nakedness, her boss knelt with his thighs parted, exposing his semi-erect cock. Her pulse skittered at the picture he made, with his skin bare for her touch while the red sleep mask rested over his eyes, a brilliant contrast to the dark creaminess of his body.

"I see you've decided to stay, slave." She sat down on the settee, her gaze hungry.

"Yes, Mistress." His response wasn't the meekest she'd ever heard, but he seemed comfortable enough for a man in his position.

"Good. Before we start, do you have a safeword?" She swung her leg over the edge of settee.

"Ah...no. Do I need one?" He tipped his head.

"Yes. Never scene without one, slave. Until you can decide upon a personal one, why don't we go with the word 'red'? It's a classic stop word that any

Domme worth her salt will recognize and halt without question."

He nodded. "Yes, Mistress."

Shifting her weight forward, she studied him. "Limits. What boundaries will you not cross? If I told you I wanted to bind you, flog you, have you eat my pussy before I shove an anal plug up your tight ass, what would you say?" She studied him.

Wyk's tongue peeked out to touch the top of his lip, before darting back in, his nostrils flared. "Where do I sign up, Mistress?" His chest expanded and between his thighs his cock filled until it lay thick with a slight curve against his stomach. She focused on his words to resist the urge to move to his side so she could touch the straining length.

"So you're not opposed to a bit of pain with your sex?" She toyed with the lashes on the flogger.

"No, Mistress." He licked his lower lip this time. "I once had a girlfriend who loved to smack my ass when I got out of the shower. She never did understand why I chased her around the bathroom, afterward, then pinned her to any hard surface I could find, so I could fuck her."

She squirmed against the cushion and pushed the image Wyk had painted away. "And what about eating pussy? Not every man enjoys it, but it's something I will demand. Will I have a fight on my hands in order to feel your tongue on my clit?"

A low groan escaped Wyk's chest. "Only if you try to push me away before you come, Mistress."

She chuckled at his response. "If I decide to give you the gift of my orgasm, slave, it is my choice. You should be thankful if I allow you to sip at my folds."

"And I will be, Mistress. Just don't expect me to be happy if you take away my treat before I'm done."

He shifted a bit on his knees.

"So you don't mind pain with your sex, you love oral sex, but what about anal? I brought a plug with me—one that has never been used—and unless you call it one of your hard limits, I will shove up it your tight ass before the night is done."

"Ah...." He cleared his throat a couple of times, but Venus could be patient now that she had him. "Let's just say I wouldn't be averse to it, Mistress."

"Not adverse to it? Does that mean you'll tolerate the plug, or that you'll beg me for more?"

Wyk hesitated. "I honestly don't know, Mistress. I've had nothing back there bigger than my pinkie or my last girlfriend's tongue."

She walked over to her bag to retrieve the plug. "Good to know." She took it out of its unopened package then rinsed the supple silicone in the small sink in the wet bar. Then she returned to his side and squatted down in front of him. "Hold your hands out for me."

He jumped a bit at her order, but obeyed. "Yes, Mistress."

Breaking one of her own rules and knowing he couldn't see her, she smiled. After placing the plug between his palms, she grabbed the small remote. She resisted the urge to flip it on—to see if he'd jump again, or perhaps make that sexy sound of need.

Wyk tried to measure the plug's dimensions. Not overly large, but thicker than anything he'd ever taken back there. Perhaps if he asked her nicely, she'd use plenty of lube before attempting to shove it up his ass. A sudden vibration caused him to fumble the device.

"Don't drop it, slave. I shall be disappointed if

you break my toy within the first few minutes of the scene." The vibration grew more intense, but this time he was prepared. He wrapped his fingers around it as the pulse of the toy radiated up his arms. His cock dripped from excitement. What would this feel like inside of him? He'd once used a vibrator in the ass of a former girlfriend who enjoyed double penetration. The feel of it against the underside of his cock had driven him crazy. The idea of her doing the same teased him. Would she be experienced enough with the toy to find his prostate? Or would the vibration be too much for him if she let him fuck her at the same time? Anticipation of finding out grew inside him until he wanted shove the plug up his own ass.

"Good, slave, don't let go of the plug. I want you to feel what later will be inside of you." Her voice came from the left. "But first...." Her fingernails lightly scratched over his scalp." There's a small matter of your early arrival to deal with."

"Yes, Mistress." He wouldn't argue with her. If she wanted to abuse his body, he had no issue with it. Particularly if she choose to use the flogger.

"How early were you, slave?" Her fingers abandoned him, before a light tap struck his shoulder.

"About twenty-five minutes, Mistress."

"Ah." She hummed near his left ear. "Under normal circumstances, I would require one stroke for every minute. However that number of lashes from the flogger would probably make you too sore to play. Nor do I want to spend the night tending your back. I want you to leave this room in the morning with a smile and a few pleasant aches."

"Yes, Mistress." He gave a sigh of relief. Twenty-five strokes with the flogger for being early? He'd remember that in the future, and either make sure he arrived on time or limit his arrival to ten minutes early.

"So instead, I want you to tell me about the last time you jacked off, slave. What you were thinking about; why you were doing it?"

He bit his lower lip. If he refused to tell her, Venus would suspect he knew it was her. But if he did, the little tyrant would be impossible to live with once they returned to work. *I'm screwed either way.* Give up the chance to be with her now, or live with her smugness when they got back to the office.

"I'm waiting. Unless you would rather have the lashes?" Her voice seemed farther away but no less firm.

"I was at work."

"You were? Such a naughty boy. And what tempted you into such behavior at your place of business?" A light thud sounded from his left. Her jean shorts?

"I was horny." *Much like I am now.*

Her chuckle surprised him. He almost expected her to put him in his place for his sarcasm. "Of course you were. But why?"

He blurted out the truth. "I have this damned assistant. All I can think about is fucking her across my desk. She orders me around at the office, tells me that I have to give her my whereabouts at all times. I'm the boss, but she acts like she's my keeper. Her demands drive me nuts."

Venus's very familiar excuse filled the air. His assistant spoke, not the Domme.

"Drives you nuts because she needs those things to do her job better, or because you think you shouldn't have to answer to a lowly assistant? Did you ever think perhaps she's trying to take care of you?"

"Take care of me? No, I think it's because she's a Domme. She has to be in control. It irritates me. I'm not a child."

She sighed. "Even children know to check in so their parents know their whereabouts, but enough of that. You didn't come here to talk about your issue with your assistant. I want to know more about why you jerked off at work. Surely it wasn't just because...this assistant was there. What did I do to cause such a response?"

He let her slip of the tongue pass. Why end the game so soon? "I picked up the phone to check on my reservations for my flight out here and accidentally overheard her conversation. She planned to get laid tonight."

"And that aroused you?" Her answer was a bit breathless. Was she rubbing her clit, masturbating to his words? The idea thrilled him, even as he wanted to push her hand aside so he could be the one pleasuring her.

"Hell, yeah. Especially when she mentioned a bag of goodies to use on him." He shifted a bit, widening his thighs to give his cock more room. "I've wanted in her bed since the moment I found out she was a Domme, but after she said she had a cock ring, and flogger for the lucky son of a bitch, I got so hard I had to have relief."

He heard another rustle before a low hum filled the room. A vibrator? He wanted to howl. He wanted to watch her pleasure herself, so he could do the same.

"So did you just whip it out there in your office?

If so, it had to have been risky. She could've walked in at any moment."

He groaned. "If only." His cock ached even more at the idea. What would prim Ms. Spinazzola-Navarro do if she caught him jerking off? Lecture him about unprofessional behavior, or maybe go all Domme on his ass? Would she rub her clit while she watched?

"No, I whipped it out in my executive bathroom, Mistress." Irritated, he made his next words as raunchy as possible. "Like a hundred times before, I imagined her there, telling me I could only come when she allowed it. I'd stroke my cock, wishing she was there to control my pleasure."

"What if she refused to let you jerk that cock to completion, slave? Instructed you to sit behind your desk with your erection tenting those pretty little trousers of yours?" The buzzing stopped. A low growl built in his chest. He wanted to see. The blindfold drove him nuts. He held the plug only to keep the game from ending.

"I would like to say I'd have stopped, if I was on the verge of orgasm and she commanded me to cease, I don't think I could've obeyed." Her scent teased his nose, and warm hands surrounded his cock and slid down his length.

"Which is exactly why you will wear this, slave."

Something tight pinched at the base of his cock. His mind whirled as the implication of it set in. A cock ring! His Mistress now controlled his pleasure.

Chapter Five

Wyk on his knees, the red mask over his eyes, and the vibrating ring cinched tight around the base of his cock made Venus's mouth water. Of course, he ruined the picture when he dropped the plug and grabbed for his groin.

"Either it stays or you leave, slave." She wouldn't allow any doubt about who was in charge of this scene to enter Wyk's devious little mind. They weren't at work now.

He groaned and dropped his fists to his thighs. He took a few deep breaths and his shoulders sagged. "May I speak, Mistress?"

"Of course. I'm not the type of Mistress who demands total obedience from her slave, to the point they are allowed to speak only when I say they can. I want to control you, not take away your choices."

His shoulders relaxed. "Does the ring mean I won't come tonight?"

Ah, so that's his issue. He thinks I'll torment him until his balls are blue then refuse to let him come.

"That all depends upon you, slave. If you're good, there will be plenty of pleasure...for both of us."

He nodded and one of his killer smiles crossed his face. "I've been told I'm really good, Mistress."

Typical Wyk. "We shall see. First you have to earn the right."

His nostrils flared. "And how do I do that?"

"By giving up that formidable self-control to me. Allowing me to do what I wish with your sexy body." She let the words sink in.

His lips parted and he nodded. "I'll try, Mistress."

"That's all I guess I can ask for at this point." She didn't have the right to demand anything more from him. *This is only for tonight.* She leaned down and snagged one of his wrists. "Up. You've been on your knees long enough, and I want to get a good look at my slave."

Her heart skipped a beat when he raised his arm, patting the air in front of him. For a split second she thought he would remove his mask.

"A hand up, Mistress?"

"Of course." She hooked her arms through his to help him to his feet. For once she was happy for her larger than average size, for the height she'd cursed her parents for since the day she grew taller than the average woman. It gave her submissive something to hang onto, to rely upon. She inhaled when his cock brushed her shorts. She hadn't changed into the Domme clothing she'd selected for their date, but she wouldn't read too much into that. Instead she would explore the delicious body in front of her. She ran her hands over his warm chest, then teased his nipples. She loved how the little black disks pebbled under her touch.

"Sensitive?" She knew the answer but wanted him to admit it.

"Yes, Mistress." His breath teased her temple.

"Ever had them clamped?" She pinched them between her forefingers and thumbs.

"No, Mistress." He gasped, thrusting his chest into her palms.

She sucked one of the nubs between her lips, licking and nipping at the captured flesh. He clutched the back of her head.

"Hands down! You don't touch me without permission, slave."

Against her stomach, his cock jerked. "I'm sorry, Mistress." His arms dropped to his sides.

"Not as sorry as you will be. Hands behind your back." She leaned over and snagged the Velcro cuffs from the toy bag. "Since it's obvious you love topping from the bottom, we will nip this behavior in the bud." She circled him, and attached one cuff to his thick wrist. "These beginner restraints, shouldn't be too uncomfortable, but they will keep you from touching without permission." Once the other one was on, she pinched his fingers. When the blood rushed back into them, she did the same to his other hand. "How's that? Too tight?"

His voice trembled. "No, Mistress."

"Good. And your safe word?" She returned to her former position in front of him.

"Red, Mistress." His chest heaved, and his cock wept drops of clear fluid. One of them coursed down his shaft and tempted her. She wanted to taste. His reaction to being restrained and at her mercy pleased her.

"Correct. If this gets to be too much, I want you to use it." She fell to her knees and sucked his cock deep inside her mouth. At his hoarse shout, she smiled with her mouth full. Some Dommes considered this act subservient, but she got a thrill like no other. With Wyk tied up like a Thanksgiving turkey, she could choose to give him pleasure or pain. The feeling went straight to her head.

"Mistress!" He swayed into her mouth, his hips

bucking. Wrapping her fist around him above the cock ring, she pulled back, tracing the vein on the underside as she retreated. She lapped at the head, then sucked it inside her mouth. Not only did he smell divine, he tasted just as good. She could become addicted to his flavor. Not that she would ever tell him that. As she explored him, she ignored his praise, his babbling pleas. He was hers—at least for the moment—and she would enjoy him.

Wyk's world centered on the hot mouth and sleek tongue tormenting his dick. He'd never expected to feel her mouth around him without an inordinate amount of pleas on his part. But Venus surprised him as she tried to suck his soul out through the head of his cock. The lash of her tongue, the tight suction of her lips, and even the scrape of her teeth pushed him higher, until he hung on the edge of release. The cock ring kept him from going off like a short-fused cannon when something brushed his anus. When she pushed in a finger, he jerked as if a strong jolt of electricity had hit him.

"Mistress! Please!" The slight stretching inflamed his desire and he tightened down. His dazed thoughts went to the plug he'd dropped earlier.

"Shh, relax for me, slave. I don't want to tear you. It's only me for the moment. No plug." She whispered the words against his inner thigh, her breath teasing him.

"Ah...I'll try." He had to force himself to relax, to allow her access to such a vulnerable part of his body. Within seconds, however, she pressed deeper and rubbed against his prostate. A jolt of sensation hit him hard.

"There it is." Her smug tone washed over him. "Does it feel good when I do this?" She pushed a bit harder, then circled her finger. He groaned as a bomb detonated inside him. Pleasure, sharp and brutal, swept over him.

"Son of a...please...fuck...." The pleasure buffeted him with each rotation, even though the torture device at the base of his dick wouldn't allow him to come.

"Hmmm." She lapped at the slit of his cockhead. "Obviously it does. Perhaps, if you're good, I'll do it again...when you don't have the cock ring on." Then she abandoned his ass and released his cock. He wanted to cry. At least, until she hooked her arm around his neck to press her lips to his. He groaned at the taste of himself on her tongue when she took total possession of their kiss as she had everything else since he'd entered the room. He swayed on his feet by the time she released him.

"Damned if you don't taste good, slave." She sounded a bit hoarse, but he wouldn't gloat and risk her withdrawal.

"More, Mistress." He didn't care if he had to beg.

"And more is what you shall get." She led him by his cock. "There is an ottoman front of you, slave. I'll turn you around and then I want you to sit down. Do you understand?"

"Yes, Mistress." The lightly textured fabric of the ottoman tickled his bare ass after he settled in position. He wanted to wiggle, but all thoughts of that slipped his mind when she crawled onto his lap and straddled his hips. Her shorts rubbed against him. It drove him mad to know that all that separated his cock from her pussy was a layer of denim.

"You mentioned you like to eat pussy, but first I

want to see how talented your lips are. Open." The pebbled tip of her breast brushed his cheek.

He turned his face to capture her nipple in his mouth, sucking her while she held the back of his head to guide him. When she pulled away, he growled and tried to follow. His reward was to be guided to her other breast to find a captive nipple ring through it. He latched on and flicked its stiffness before curling his tongue around the ring and tugging. Her soft mewl filled his ears. Uncertain of her response, he pinched her flesh with his teeth. Her groan followed a harsh demand for more, which he gladly gave. He licked, nibbled, and sucked whatever part of her breasts she pressed against his mouth.

"Enough." Her weight lifted from his lap. "You've proved your point, slave, but I'm too hot to appreciate your mouth."

Panting, he waited for her to continue, to explain. Surely she wouldn't abandon him. "Mistress?"

"I need to feel this...." Her hand found his cock. "Inside of me. Would you enjoy that, slave?"

"Fuck, yeah." His head tipped back as her grip tightened before she released him.

"That's not a proper answer, slave." The unexpected slap of the flogger against his back sent another jolt of pleasure through him. A hiss escaped him; heat raced across his skin. "Care to reword your answer?"

"Fuck, yeah, Mistress?" He gritted between his teeth, jerking against his bonds. Not that he wanted out of them. He needed to pit his strength against the cuffs that held him, to know that he couldn't escape. The flogger thudded against his left shoulder. Its strands wrapped over the top of it so the ends hit his collarbone. More heat followed when she gave his other shoulder the same treatment. Within seconds she found a steady rhythm, which had his back as hot as his desire for more.

"I should make you ask nicely, slave. Make you beg to feel my pussy around you." Her words were cold, but he could hear the intensity behind them.

"I'm sorry, Ven...Mistress. Please fuck me." With lust singing though him, he almost spoke her name. He'd die if she didn't give him what he needed. He'd crawl across the floor on his knees, let her collar him like a pup, anything to have her finish what she'd started.

Chapter Six

Venus held the flogger in one fist as she stared down at him. She could only hope his desire for her had reached its peak, because she couldn't wait much longer. His breath was fast, and every so often his hips rocked up. The idea that she, Venus Spinazzola-Navarro, had pushed the great and mighty Wyk Havas to this point stroked her own desire higher. Her blood raced in her veins. Still, she'd caught his slip. How had he known? She'd thought the shadows had hidden her identity, but perhaps they hadn't. Now torn, did she finish this? Or back off? Logic said she should let him free and send him on his merry way, but the dominant part of her wanted what she'd created. When he released another moan, his distress registered on her lust-dazed senses, and she decided to hang onto the illusion as long as she could, because tomorrow he'd be gone.

"Better answer, slave." She pulled a condom from her pocket. "I'm going to remove the cock ring, for a moment, to put on a condom on you. Do not come."

She crouched between his thighs, ripped open the wrapper with her teeth. After pulling the sheath out, she rolled it down the swollen length of his shaft. Meeting his eyes, she tugged on the quick release snap. He groaned above her head, his torso twisting.

A quick glance at his groin surprised her as he seemed to swell before her eyes. *Damn, that baby looks ready to burst.* "Do you think you can last long enough for your Mistress to find her pleasure?"

His chest heaved, and he shook his head. "Too close, Mistress. Put it back on. I have to last as long as you need."

Surprise filtered through her. She'd expected him to brag about his stamina, not to ask for a return of the ring. Her heart melted a bit. "Fine." She re-snapped the device, then checked to make sure it wasn't pinching anything important. She rose to her feet. Yanking the tank top the rest of the way off, she dropped it to the floor before reaching for the snap on her shorts. She ripped open the fastening and shucked her shorts and panties in one smooth move. Dammit, if this was the only time she would get to fuck him, she wouldn't waste it by having half of her clothing on.

"For honesty, slave, you get a small reward." Delving inside her wet pussy, she gathered her juices and painted his lips with them. "Suck."

His tongue curled around her finger and tugged it inside the hot cavern of his mouth. "Mmmm."

When she drew away, he groaned. "You taste so good, Mistress, that all I want to do is eat your pussy." His panted as she climbed back on his lap, this time facing away from him.

"Later," she promised as she centered herself over his cock. Pressing the head into her opening, she lowered her body onto his shaft. She groaned as his thick length stretched her. It had been so long since she'd taken a man inside her, and he was long and hard. It took several long minutes before she sank all the way down on him. The room filled with her gasps and her slave's groans.

"So tight, Mistress." His breath puffed over her shoulder. He rocked upward, sliding along her sensitive tissues.

"You fill me," she agreed. Using her strong legs for balance, she began to slowly ride him, careful not to buck too hard and knock him off the ottoman. Ever-spreading tingles buffeted her each time she rose and sank. She needed more, but her sadistic nature wanted, no needed to drag it out. Against her neck, his heavy pants teased her sensitive skin.

"Please, Mistress." His lips skittered over the base of her neck. Gooseflesh raced down her arms, coaxing her need higher when he sucked on the flesh.

"No hickies, slave. My boss will ask questions." She bounced a bit faster at his growl, but slowed once more when he moved with her. "Be still. Let me have my fun."

He froze and for a second, Venus though he would dump her from her perch, but he didn't. Instead he braced his legs and leaned back enough to give her more room to move. "As you will, Mistress." The words were tight with need.

Then she unleashed her inner Domme, riding him slow, then fast, then back again until he writhed under her. His chest heaved against her back, and his groans were raw. Her body trembled on the edge, but she refused to go over without him. She would not be alone in her release. Her slave would come with her. She slammed down one more time, before she slipped forward enough to reach the cock ring.

"God damnit, Venus, finish it." His nostrils flared and he nipped her shoulder.

She froze, the reality of what they were doing hit her. It wasn't Mistress V fucking her sub, it was

Venus. "Ah...."

"Don't you dare stop!" He bucked under her and rubbed across her G-spot. "Because, so help me God, if you do, when I get free I'll hunt your sexy ass down and fuck you 'til you can't walk."

She snarled at him as she wrenched open the snap on his cock ring, then braced herself on his knees. "Like hell you will. Damn topping-from-the-bottom bastard. I'll show you," she gritted out. Her fingers dug into his legs as she rode him fast and hard. Behind her, he groaned.

"Shit...I'm gonna...can I come, Mistress?"

Unable to delay her own orgasm any longer, she gave in. "Come for me, slave."

Under her, he bucked up, only her forward weight on his legs kept them from toppling off the ottoman. His wild bucks sent her careening over the edge. Vicious pleasure battered her as she clung to his knees.

The room rang with their shouts of completion.

***

The sun had begun to peek over the horizon when Venus woke. Her hand patted the cool spot on the bed next to her and she sighed. Opening her eyes, she took stock of her surroundings. Her body ached pleasantly from her night with Wyk, but as she'd expected, he was gone. The red sleep mask that rested on the pillow next to hers was the only indication the night had been real. She touched the edge of it with fingers that trembled. It was hard to believe it was over. Especially after the experience they'd shared.

After their first explosive mating, neither had let

the illusion of their time together drop. She'd uncuffed him and led him to her bedroom, where they'd spent almost the entire night making love. She'd been in control each and every time they came together. *Except for the last time.* Hazy memories of waking face down and on her knees as Wyk slowly joined their bodies, sent a weak spurt of desire through her. *He was so gentle, I didn't even protest.* She stilled at the thought. *But now it's over.*

Her glorious one-night stand had been everything she'd hoped it would be, her body sated to the point she shouldn't want sex for a while. *Well at least not until Wyk walks into the room.* She'd have to remember to write an e-mail to thank Madame Eve when she got home—after she got done crying. This little venture had cost her more than the money she'd paid for Madame Eve's exclusive services. When she returned to Chicago, she'd be in the market for a new job, because she wouldn't be able to work under him now. Sure, she'd give her two weeks' notice; she couldn't leave her boss high and dry. However, she didn't think she could watch the parade of women resume—not that there had been many, in the past few months since her confession.

As she kicked the blankets off, the door to the bedroom opened. Wyk, in just his exercise shorts, walked in. The sight of all his dark skin distracted her from the breakfast tray in his hands. But when he set his burden down between them. Belgian waffles, crispy bacon and fluffy scrambled eggs filled the air with their heavenly aromas. Her mouth watered.

"Madame Eve thought of everything. Even fresh-squeezed orange juice." He smiled, his dimple flashing. "The manager brought it up along with this for both of us."

She hesitated for a moment, before reaching for the crisp buff envelope between their plates. The flap fell loose.

"You opened it?"

He handed her a glass of juice. "Yes. Why don't you eat, while I grab a shower, Mistress?" He pressed a quick kiss to her temple then disappeared into the bathroom.

She couldn't help but stare as mist drifted through the open door. Perhaps he shared her love of hot showers as well, but the thought didn't comfort her. Instead his easy acceptance and nonchalance as he brought her breakfast in bed pissed her off.

"How the hell can he act as if he didn't rock my world last night? Does he honestly think he can use me to scratch his itch then have everything return to normal this morning? That I will just let him jump in my shower like nothing happened, so he can go on his merry way?" Her ire at the situation continued to build when she heard him singing—of all things—as he washed away the evidence of their night together.

She opened the envelope, to keep from strangling the man. Lucky they would go their separate ways. She'd end up killing him if they stayed together. How could she ever have believed he could be the one for her when he acted this way? It hurt her to think he hadn't experienced the same connection she had.

She stared down at the heavy stationary. She expected to find a standard thank you from 1Night Stand and a referral card to give to a friend. Instead, she found three words scrawled in a feminine hand.

Believe—Madame Eve

Her jaw dropped. How had the woman known she would doubt the connection between her and

Wyk? Completely freaked, she lunged from the bed. She had to leave *now*.

***

As he dried off, Wyk whistled softly. He'd never felt better. After a night of passionate lovemaking that had rocked him to the core, he'd woken up wrapped around his Mistress's lush form. Despite the fact neither of them had gotten more than three hours of sleep, he felt like a million bucks—like he could take on the world single-handed. Especially since, when he'd called down to order their breakfast, the manager had agreed to extend their stay through the weekend.

Now he had to convince his Mistress to spend the rest of the weekend together in Vegas. They could use their time together, between bouts of loving, to figure out the logistics of continuing their relationship when they returned to Chicago. He would never let Venus get away from him. He'd transfer her to another department if she didn't want to work under him anymore. He wouldn't give up his Mistress. She'd filled the hole inside of him with her dominant but loving nature. Something he would never find on any corner.

Wyk studied his reflection as he shaved his face and head. He'd swiped her razor, but he didn't think she'd mind, since he used it to keep him tidy like she'd asked. The rest of his toilette didn't take long because he didn't plan on leaving the suite anytime soon. He wandered out into the bedroom, nude. After their night together, he had nothing to hide. Perhaps, he'd finally get his mouth on her pretty little cunt. He'd been good, really good. *Well other than the last time, but she'd just too tempting, all she snuggled down into the sheets.*

He froze in the doorway when he found Venus throwing things into her overnight case, dressed in the same outfit she'd worn the night before. Panic rushed through him. Had she had second thoughts while he showered?

"Mistress, what are you doing?"

Her head flew up. "Don't call me that! I'm not...." Her eyes darted away as she slammed the lid shut on the case. "I have to get out of here."

"Why? We don't have to be back to work until Monday. Which reminds me we need to talk." He crossed his arms over his chest.

"I know." She shoved her feet into her shoes. "I'll e-mail you."

Frustration rocked him. "What do you mean you'll e-mail me?"

She looked up. "My resignation. Then we can forget this ever happened—"

"Red." He whispered the word just loud enough for her to hear.

She gave him a confused glance. "Excuse me?"

He stalked her until he had her pinned up against the bed. His slight shove sent her tumbling onto the mattress. Before she could scramble away, he followed her down. "You said 'red' stops everything."

She nodded, her face flushed. "Yeah, it does."

"Good. Then I'm calling 'red' right now. You can't run from this. From me."

Licking her lips, she gazed up at him. "I can't?"

"No. You may be my Mistress, I may even let you control our sex life, but I'm a possessive bastard. I won't let you go because you're worried about what others think." He nuzzled her neck. "Believe in us."

She nibbled on her lower lip. "This isn't something your friends and family will understand or even accept. I want to collar you, Wyk. To place my mark at your throat. This isn't a game to me. Or some kink I enjoy from time to time. This is my reality. If you accept my collar, I will own you—body, heart, and soul."

His heart turned over at her words. After snagging the tray, the one they were damned lucky they hadn't spilled when they landed on the bed, he tugged the thin collar out from under the plate cover. He pressed it into her palm. When her beautiful green eyes lit up, he closed her fingers around the leather that would mark him as hers.

"You already own me, Mistress. All you have to do is believe." Then he tipped his head to offer his throat. Seconds dragged by as he waited. Had he gotten through her stubborn head he was where he wanted to be?

It seemed to take forever but he felt the slide of leather against his skin as she fastened the collar in place. Peace settled over him. "Thank you, Mistress." His fingers found the small metal tag and the letters engraved on it.

"Believe, huh?" She whispered the word and brushed his hand aside. She studied the tag for a moment, then her eyes met his. "Very appropriate. I wonder how she knew."

"Don't know, but I'm glad she did." He dipped his head until their noses touched. "I believe in us. Can you, Mistress?"

Her answer came in the form of a physical caress. He groaned when she scratched his scalp with her nails. His eyes drifted shut as the sting went straight to his dick.

"Looks like I don't have much choice, do I? Considering my slave has already told me I can't run from him."

"No running." He shook his head. "It's my hard limit," he gasped when her fingers dug into his shoulders.

"Then I suggest you thank me with that mouth of yours, slave. I want to see if you're as good as you say you are." She nipped his lower lip and gave his shoulders a shove.

"Does that mean you want me to eat your pussy, Mistress?" He settled between her splayed thighs and slipped his hands under her ass.

"Almost as much as you do." She cupped the back of his head and pushed him closer to her wet folds. "Now eat me. Or it will be ten lashes from the crop for you."

Happiness filled him. This was exactly what he wanted. "Yes, Mistress."

The End

Dakota Trace

Kotori's Sacrifice

A Dominant who just couldn't let go....

As an experienced Dom, Seba Havas, specializes in helping traumatized submissives find the release they need. He knows when a firm hand is needed or a gentle touch will work better, but nothing in his nearly fifteen years in the scene prepares him for Akira. Like a whirlwind, she turns his orderly life upside down with her refusal to submit. Still reeling from his failure with her six months later, he turns to 1Night Stand. Madame Eve's suggestion? A trip to the Carnivore Club, the brand new BDSM themed Las Vegas Strip resort on a date to an elegant masquerade ball with a beautiful submissive.

A submissive who's willing to sacrifice it all....

As the oldest daughter of the Ito clan, Akira has been responsible and self-controlled her entire life, up to the point it has caused her to lose the dominant she loves. Now she has one chance left to prove to Seba she can be what he needs. In true Vegas fashion, and with a little help from Madame Eve, she's going to gamble it all on one night of dominance and submission. But will it be enough?

Chapter One

"*D*o *you need more, kotori? Or are you ready to fly for me?" Leaning in to whisper into the bound submissive's ear, Seba brushed his lips against the delicate curve as his cock throbbed against his leathers. It'd taken a great deal of time, but he'd finally managed to push the lush Japanese woman to the edge of her control. Something she'd warned him would never happen when she'd admitted she wanted to submit.*

"Please, Sensei, I can't." Her dark chocolate eyes sparkled with unshed tears when she turned her head to make eye contact with him. Bound to the St. Andrew's Cross in the middle of LRA's main playroom, it was the only portion of her body she could shift.

"Why not?" He trailed the butt of his whip across the ivory shoulder sporting a tiny, vibrant hummingbird tattoo. "What are you afraid of?"

"I...." She bit her lower lip—something she only did when she lied. Then he saw her withdrawing once again. "I...don't know." Her lashes drifted shut, hiding her gaze from him.

A low growl built in his chest. Tired of her games, his frustration simmered just under his skin. She'd come to him, begged him to push her past the rigid control she couldn't seem to let go of. Yet, she still fought and lied to avoid the very thing she claimed to want.

"Hiding again?"

With his free hand, he popped one of the cheeks of her ass left bare by the leather thong she wore. "What is our first rule, Akari?"

She drew a ragged breath. "I will look at Sensei every time we speak unless otherwise directed."

"And our second?"

"I will speak the truth, Sensei."

"Yet you deliberately defy me at every turn. Lowering your eyes. Lying, when you know I can read your deception like an open book." He drew back. "One would think you don't wish to continue with our agreement."

"No....." The first hint of true emotion crossed her face. Her lips trembled. "I'll do better. I swear, Sensei."

He flinched at the soft honorific only she had ever used. A boon from when they'd first negotiated their contract, much like him calling her little bird. At first, he'd thought the Japanese words would put her at ease—something from her homeland— something familiar. Now, he realized, they were nothing more than another shield for her to hide behind.

"You keep promising me, but so far I've seen no real effort." He shook his head. "In fact, I don't think you have any intention of doing better." He coiled up the short whip, slipping it over a hook attached to his belt. Gazing at the slender red collar around her throat, he sighed. "I'm beginning to think I'm not the right master for you."

"Don't do this, please, Sensei." Tears spilled over her flushed cheeks. "Don't give up on me...."

"Yo, Seb! You in here? Mistress says the taxi for the airport is on its way."

Jerked out of the torturous memories leading up to the un-collaring of his last submissive, Seba Havas turned to face his beaming younger brother. A welcome interruption, his brother stood in the open doorway of the guest bedroom. At twenty-five, Wyk had found *the* woman who could satisfy him to hell and back. *All at the hands of the mysterious Madame Eve.* The same woman he'd put his confidence in after Wyk returned from Vegas wearing his assistant's collar.

"Yeah, I can't believe I let you talk me into using this matchmaker, but if she worked for you, what do I have—"

"To lose?" Appearing in the hallway behind Wyk, Venus joined her submissive. White, curvy, and a few inches shorter than Wyk, she was the perfect foil for his six-foot-four, darker-than-the-ace-of-spades brother. Venus radiated dominance. "One can only hope she can help change that long face you've been carrying around for the past six months. Besides, the Carnivore Club resort is reported to have the finest in leather and steel."

"So does LRA, if fine quality is all I need," Seba replied, referring to the club where both he and Venus had memberships.

Venus propped her hands on her hips. "So it does. Everything—including Akari."

Seba stiffened, but like an addict needing his next fix, he couldn't help but ask. "She's found a new Dom?"

"Don't do this to yourself, Seb," Wyk pleaded, looking from Seba to his Mistress and back again.

"No, he needs to know." Venus placed her hand on Wyk's shoulder. "She scened with Randy last night."

Seba's heart sank. One of his best friends and the club's most in-demand dominant, Randy could give her what she needed. "I see. He's a good choice. Firm, but caring."

"She didn't—" Wyk tried to comfort him.

"Enough, Wyk." Venus swatted his ass. "The doorman just called up. Seba's cab is here. Why don't you carry his bags down?"

Wyk looked ready to argue, but held his tongue when Venus gave him a pointed look. After the door shut behind his brother, Venus turned back to him. "Look, I know you're struggling right now, but you can't keep ignoring your needs. Go to Vegas. Check out the club. Enjoy yourself, and for once, quit worrying about what is going on with that little Asian tart who has you tied up in knots. Give Madame Eve a chance. She knows her stuff."

Seba gave her a half-ass grin. "I think you might be partial, but thanks for the pep talk." He leaned in and brushed a kiss across her cheek. "Worry about keeping my brother in line while I'm gone. I want a business to come back to."

She laughed. "Darlin', it's what I do best."

***

After landing in Vegas, Seba piled into the hotel shuttle, along with several other tourists on their way to the flagship hotel of the Castillo Hotels and Resorts chain. Shutting out the excited chatter of his fellow passengers, he stared out the window at the bright, flashing Vegas lights. Instead, he focused on his upcoming date. The folded papers inside the pocket of his suit jacket held all the pertinent information about the submissive Madame Eve had set him up with. *Well, other than her name.* The woman's request for anonymity didn't surprise him. After all, they would be meeting at the grand opening of an underground BDSM club. He couldn't expect her to want to broadcast her identity.

"Okay, folks, we're here." The shuttle driver steered into the circular drive in front of the hotel.

Seba exited and waited for the driver to pop the rear hatch. After grabbing his overnight bag and the plain black duffel holding his toys, he headed toward the entrance, distracted when his cell phone vibrated at his hip.

Unclipping the device, he saw he had two new texts. Thumbing through the first, he shook his head. Wyk wanted to know if he'd landed and made it to the hotel yet. Since his brother had set up his reservations, he should've expected the little snoop would want feedback. He sent back a quick reply that he'd arrived but hadn't checked in yet. Then he moved on to the second text. A reminder from Madame Eve that the costume for the masquerade party where he'd be meeting his date would be delivered no later than eight o'clock. After texting a thank you, he snapped his phone shut and sighed. How the hell had he gotten himself into this mess? Why couldn't Akira have been what he needed?

***

Standing with a crowd of Japanese tourists near the fountain inside the lobby of the Vegas Castillo Hotel and Resort, Akira Ito caught her breath when

Seba stopped to check his phone. Even wearing rumpled clothing from his flight, his broad shoulders, trim waist, and close-cropped dark hair made her want to fall to her knees—to offer her submission. She'd fucked up the last time they'd been together. The second the lie passed her lips, she'd known better. He'd warned her time and time again about her evasiveness and little white lies. *But I didn't expect him to remove my collar and tell me he no longer wanted to be my Dom.*

Her fingers went to her bare throat. After wearing the choker for the short six weeks she'd served him, she shouldn't have grown quite so attached to it. Or still be missing its presence almost six months later. But she did. Almost as much as she missed touching all of his luscious chocolate skin. Watching him walk across the lobby, she wanted to go to him, to beg him to take her back. Hell, she'd even try to explain why she found it so hard to let go. She closed her eyes for a moment, reminding herself it wasn't the time. Madame Eve had given her explicit instructions. She couldn't approach Seba until the masquerade tonight.

"Miss Ito?" A tall, immaculately dressed man appeared next to her. He held out his hand. "My name is Jackson Castillo, and I'd like to welcome you to our hotel."

"Thank you." She shook his hand, amazed he'd sought her out. A personal touch for a man in his position. "If you greet everyone this way, it's no surprise you do well."

"Indeed." He smiled, revealing startling-white teeth. "However, today I've been asked by a very close friend of mine to give you a gift. Madame Eve has quite the treat for you. If you'll follow me, you have an appointment at our hair salon followed by another at our spa. I'll have your bags delivered to your room."

Her mind whirled. She'd spent a huge chunk of her savings on her 1Night Stand date. Judging by the decor in the lobby, there would be no way she could afford the pampering he suggested, and still be able to eat. "But I didn't set up—"

"Nonsense. Consider this a perk. A part, if you will, of your date-night package. Madame Eve has taken care of all the details." He squeezed her shoulder. "Much like the costume you requested, she has provided for everything during your stay. All you need is to relax and let her work her magic."

She nibbled on her lower lip. "Well, I guess it would be rude to refuse."

Jackson chuckled. "Of course, it would be." He held out his arm. "Shall we go?"

Pasting a pleasant expression on her face, she took his arm. "Lead the way, Mr. Castillo."

***

A few hours later, every part of her had been scrubbed, peeled, plucked, and lotioned until she glowed. They'd even waxed her pussy hair, until only a small triangle remained at the top of her mound. They had then colored the swatch to match the new vibrant burgundy red of her formerly ebony hair. To her surprise, she hadn't gotten many weird looks when a uniformed staff member had escorted her from the salon to the spa. In fact, they passed several other people with unusual hairdos and a few who might be in costumes along the way. *Perhaps they're having an anime or Comic-Con at the hotel this weekend.*

After kicking off her shoes, she curled her toes into the plush carpet of her suite. She couldn't stop giggling at the sparkly nail polish the pedicurist had applied. She'd never worn anything but soft, pale pink. Heaven forbid the heiress to the Ito fortune be caught doing anything scandalous. "Like it really matters now," she muttered. "Considering what little money Father didn't throw away at the craps table, he squandered on loose women and American liquor."

She laid her garment bag across the bed. Anticipation built in her stomach. She couldn't believe her recklessness, but she couldn't throw away what would be her final chance to resume her place in Seba's life. *If it takes dressing up like his favorite manga character, I'll do it—red hair, guns, and all.* Self-conscious, she tucked a lock the colorist had somehow managed to perfectly match to Mey-rin's, behind her ears. Overwhelmed, she sank down on the soft mattress. Even though the stylist had assured her it was temporary, it would still take a week to ten days to wash out. She expected to get more than a few strange glances when she returned to Chicago, but it would be worth it if she wore Seba's collar.

B-R-RING.

The phone's sudden jangle startled her out of her thoughts. Reaching over, she picked up the handset.

"Hello?"

"I see you made it safe and sound." Venus's calm voice on the other end of the phone settled her nerves, as it always had.

"Yes. I just got back from the spa. All I can say is your brother-in-law had better appreciate this. Because I let them wax and color parts of me no good girl should ever allow."

A low grumble carried over the line. "This is about you shedding your good-girl image and letting your inner bad girl come out and play, Akira. There is no condemning father there to scold you, no tutor to rap your knuckles. However, if you act bratty, don't be surprised if Seb warms your ass."

She flushed and squirmed against the satin duvet at the thought. "Like you never hit me." She sighed. "But, even if I earn a punishment from this little stunt, it'll be worth it."

"What if you don't get your man?"

Akira's heart ached at the suggestion. "If Seba decides to walk away, I can always tell myself I tried."

"There's nothing wrong with trying." Venus paused. "I want you to do me a favor, well actually two. First, Wyk's begging for a picture of you in your Mey-rin getup, and second...forget about the serious, uptight teenager I met all those years ago, when your dad hired me to tutor you. She's gone. You've grown up. Instead, be the woman, the submissive, I know lurks deep inside of you. Let the rest of the world be damned. Can you do that for me?"

"I'll try," Akira whispered, blinking away her tears.

"No, you'll do more than try. You will succeed— or I'll paddle your ass myself when you return. Nothing ventured...."

"Nothing gained." She gripped the receiver, praying her courage wouldn't desert her.

Chapter Two

A loud knock startled Seba awake. Lying on one of the most comfortable beds he could ever remember sleeping in, he yawned. Disoriented, he blinked then groaned when his sleep-dazed mind recognized the beautiful suite.

Vegas. My date. Damned masquerade ball.

He pushed up on one arm and stared at the mantel clock above the fireplace. Ten minutes to eight. He'd only planned to rest his eyes for a moment, but slept several hours.

"Mr. Havas?" The voice filtered through the door.

"Yeah, I'm coming. Give me a second." He scrubbed his palms over his face then swung his legs off the bed and headed across the room.

He yawned once more, trying to shake the cobwebs while opening the door. A uniformed bellhop offered him a dark-maroon garment bag.

"Mr. Castillo asked me to bring this to you. He also wanted you to know the limo taking you and your date to the masquerade will be out front at nine o'clock."

Seba nodded, taking the garment bag. "Thank Mr. Castillo for his thoughtfulness." After giving the young man a generous tip, he sent him on his way.

Hanging the garment bag on a hook in the bedroom, he noticed a crisp white envelope nestled in a clear, zippered pouch. Intrigued, he tugged out a midnight-blue invitation with ivory lettering.

You are cordially invited to the Sins of the Angel Masquerade Ball
Being held at the Carnivore Club from 10:00 p.m. until 2:00 a.m.
The general mixer will start at 10 p.m., with the doors opening at 9:30 p.m.
.Hors d'oeuvres and sparkling wine will be served until 11:30 p.m., and the playroom will open for play at midnight.

The loose piece of white vellum inserted into the invitation crinkled between his fingers. Seba scanned it.

While you're our guest, we have some simple rules we'd like you to abide by. They are as follows:

During the masquerade:
All masks must remain in place.
No real names may be used. We will refer to our guests by their characters' names.
Non-alcoholic beverages are available and recommended for those who plan to play later.

After the Masquerade:
The dungeon monitors, who may be identified by their gold vests—male—or gold corsets—female— will be available throughout the evening. They are charged to refuse admittance to the playroom to any guests who appear intoxicated. They are charged with ensuring a pleasurable and safe evening for all.

> *Normal club rules will be enforced. Respect our house safewords: Red for stop and yellow for slow down.*
> *No one shall play without signed waivers and checklists.*
> *Condoms are a must. There will be no exceptions.*
> *The playroom will close at 3:00 a.m. in consideration.*
> *The resort shuttle service will be available for those not staying on the premises.*

After scanning the rules, he growled. While he'd expected the playroom rules, he hadn't anticipated the masquerade restrictions. No names? Staying in character? He eyed the garment bag.

"Well, chicken shit, open it and find out what costume Madame Eve picked out for you. Let's pray she doesn't have a macabre sense of humor and decided you'd look good in a slave costume or some pimp getup."

Sliding the zipper down, he opened the bag. At first glance, it didn't look much different than a dark suit with lots of shiny buttons. Then he spotted a note pinned to the lapel.

"Christ, another one?" he grumbled, working it free.

Seba, while it took some time for me to find the perfect costume for tonight's festivities, I do believe you'll be pleased with the one I've chosen, even if you have to forgive me for taking the liberty of making the Black Butler...well, black. Enjoy the masquerade and remember, not everything is as it seems.

Madame Eve.

An almost child-like glee washed over him. He loved manga, but how had she found out? "I can't believe she made me Sebastian Michaelis, the demon butler from the Phantomhive. How cool is that!"

Everything, from the dark, sharply creased trousers, to the brocade satin vest and the double-breasted jacket with its fancy epaulettes, spoke of the highest quality and craftsmanship. How the hell had he gotten so lucky?

Behind him, the clock struck eight. "Shit. I'm gonna be late if I don't get my ass in the shower."

***

Akira stared in the mirror. With the white lacy maid's cap over the magenta-red hair she now sported, and a formfitting black dress with a full-length ivory apron, nothing remained of the Akira Ito she knew. Paired with the thick, opaque glasses perched on her button nose, she looked like she'd walked out of the Phantomhive household. Fiddling with the long apron strings around her waist, she tried to calm her anxious nerves. Lord knew what would happen when she met up with Seba. Like her character, Mey-rin, she would flush beet red at the mere sight of him.

"I can't believe I'm doing this." She reached under her skirt to tuck the fake pistols in the holsters she'd strapped to each thigh. "Never in a million years would I have dressed up like the bumbling love interest of the most kick-ass butler in the manga world." Stepping back, she gave herself a critical eye.

Not the sexiest costume imaginable, but with its well-fitted bodice and waist-cinching snowy apron, she might be able to tempt her former Dom while still hiding her identity from Seba.

Straightening her ivory cuffs and fluffing the apron's bow, she almost jumped when her cell phone buzzed. Half expecting it to be Venus, she flipped open her phone. Instead, the text came from Madame Eve.

Remember child, nothing ventured, nothing gained. Show him you can be what he needs – Madame Eve

She drew a deep breath. Funny, how much the mystical Madame Eve reminded her of Venus.

"Speaking of Venus, I'll never hear the end of it if I don't send her the picture I promised." It took less than thirty seconds to snap a selfie and send it her friend. Then she grabbed her invitation and let herself out of her room. As she rode the elevator downstairs, she glanced at her watch. She didn't want to be late and give Seba a reason to punish her.

Although he'll probably be the one running behind. Venus swears he'll be late to his own funeral.

In the lobby, she pushed through a crowd of people dressed up in a variety of outlandish costumes. She saw everything from Nathan Fillion look-alikes to Elfin lords and warrior princesses. Evidently, she'd been wrong to assume a manga conference or even Comic-Con had overtaken the hotel. It looked more like a sci-fi convention. When two storm troopers and Spock walked by, she shook her head.

I'm supposed to find Seba in this mess?

"Miss Ito, I almost didn't recognize you." Randi, the uniformed staff member from earlier appeared next to her.

Once outside, she shivered in the cool night air. As they approached the waiting limo, the driver opened the door.

"Any sign of my date?" she asked, after the driver helped her into the warm car.

"According to the front desk, he called down a bit ago. He's running a few minutes late, but not to worry. He'll be here shortly."

Yup, Seba would be late for his own funeral.

***

Seba cursed under his breath, while waiting for the damned elevator to arrive. Tugging at his vest with one hand, he resisted the urge to snatch the heavy hairpiece off his head. The wig he'd found at the bottom of the garment bag looked great on him, but was hot. In his other hand, he held his toy bag.

"Come on, dammit. I'm already fuckin' late." He stabbed at the down arrow once more. With his suite located on the twenty-third floor, the stairs weren't an option if he didn't want to be a sweaty mess when he arrived.

Finally, the bell dinged and the doors slid open. Stepping inside, he froze. Several members of the cast from *Sailor Moon* quieted and stared at him. His palms began to sweat. After the metal doors slid shut behind him, the girls began to giggle. One brave girl, dressed in a red ruffled skirt and holding a bow and arrow—Sailor Mars, if he remembered right—stepped forward.

"Sebby, the Black Butler, right?"

"Yeah."

"So are you here for the sci-fi conference?" She

batted her fake eyelashes at him.

He shook his head. "Nope, sorry. Going to a private costume party."

She giggled. "Shame. You'd take first place in that getup." She moved closer, running her fingertips up his chest. "Are you sure we can't convince you to stay?"

He gave her a shrug. "Sorry, I already have a date."

Sticking out her lower lip, she nudged him with her hip. "Aw, come on, we're going to have an *adult* after-hours party back in my suite, once the conference entertainment is over. We were going to have the guys from *Firefly* come over, but after seeing you?" She tugged one of the buttons on his coat open. "You could be our guest of honor."

Gritting his teeth, he brushed her fingers away. "Look, I'm sure you're a bunch of sweet ladies, but—"

"Oh look, girls. Someone is playing hard to get." Sailor Mars leered at him, but with her dramatized makeup, all it did was make her look creepy.

Hefting his bag a little higher, he decided subtlety would be lost on these girls. "Frankly, ladies, I play harder than you could ever imagine. So, unless you're planning on spending half the night in bondage, with nipple clamps on your pretty little titties along with butt plugs up your asses, while I flog each of you, I suggest you look elsewhere for your guest of honor."

"But isn't that illegal in Vegas? I thought they had a law against it." The *Sailor Moon* look-alike whispered.

He gave them what he hoped was a devilish smirk. "Not anymore."

Several pairs of eyes widened, staring at him like

he'd grown a second head or threatened to eat their firstborn. When the doors opened, he gave the girls a single brief nod before entering the lobby.

Pushing through the revolving door, he almost bumped into a well-dressed man. "Oh, excuse me."

The man gave him a quick look over. "You must be Mr. Havas. I'm Randy, and Mr. Castillo asked that I make sure both you and your date made it to the limo. Sorry about the chaos inside the hotel. Sci-fi conventions can be crazy."

"As I noticed, after riding down the elevator with a bunch of frisky Sailors."

Randy blinked twice. "We have sailors in the hotel? Doesn't seem very sci-fi, but okay."

Seba laughed. "Not that kind of sailor. I'm talking about the cute young Japanese girls from the show *Sailor Moon*?"

A light bulb seemed to go on in Randy's head because he nodded. "Japanese girls aren't your thing?"

A pang in his chest at the question didn't surprise him. One Japanese girl had definitely been his thing.

Quit thinking of Akira. You have a date waiting in the car.

To cover his lapse of attention, he forced a lighthearted tone into his voice. "Not unless it's Meyrin. Something about her red hair and how innocently she blushes but still manages to be lethal does it for me."

"Perhaps a thank-you letter to the mysterious Madame Eve wouldn't be out of place. Enjoy yourselves. Your driver will wait to bring you back to the hotel after the ball."

"Of course. Thank you." He barely got the words

out before the door slammed and the car pulled away from the curb. In the darkened interior, he squinted to make out a figure sitting across from him.

His date reached over her head and a soft glow flooded the interior of the car. After his eyes adjusted to the sudden flare, his jaw about dropped to the floor while the limo picked up speed.

Wearing a formfitting black maid's uniform and a startling-snowy apron that accented her lovely tits, his bespectacled companion gave him a tentative look then stuck out her hand.

"Hello, I'm Mey-rin. I'm your date for the evening."

Chapter Three

When it became obvious he wasn't going to take her hand, Akira let hers drop. Worry chipped away at her self-confidence. Did he recognize her somehow? Maybe the costume didn't hide her identity well enough to fool him? Or could he be playing along until he got her to Carnivore Club, so he could teach her a lesson by exposing her?

"My fucking god, you're cute." He narrowed his eyes. "You look just like her."

Wetting her lips, she allowed the natural accent she'd worked so hard to lose back into her voice. "I'm very fortunate. Madame Eve found me a perfect costume. Not that yours isn't great."

The dark jacket with its shiny buttons and the ivory shirt hid a marvelous chest and abs so tight she could bounce a quarter off them. Although it would take some time to get used to the inky locks of a wig framing his dark face. She much preferred his short hair, but overall he still made her mouth water. It was a shame he wore a costume that covered all his sexy-ass tattoos. When he leaned back against the seat, she wondered if he'd let her trace them with her tongue, especially the sleek dragon that wrapped around his side. "The Black Butler, right?"

His lips quirked. "Yeah. I'm supposed to be Sebby, your love interest."

"So they say. But your costume suits you. So,

what am I to call you tonight? I know the rules say we must use our characters' first names, but, as a submissive, I find myself uncomfortable not paying you the proper respect."

Toying with one of the decorative fobs on his coat, he studied her. "While I can understand your reasoning, I ended my last relationship because my submissive hid behind similar honorifics. For now, I would prefer we go with Sir then renegotiate if we decide to scene tonight."

Placing her hands on her lap, she bowed her head. "I can live with that, Sir."

"Good." A grin tugged at his lips. "So, is this your first time in Vegas?"

"Yes. But I've heard a great deal about it. My...father visited often and loved to tell my mother and me of its great lights and wonderful shows. So when the opportunity presented itself, I thought I'd see it myself. And you?"

A thoughtful look crossed his face. "I needed a change of pace. Things back home have been tense. My last relationship...was difficult." He caught her gaze. "While I'm not the kiss-and-tell type of Dom, I do need to warn you...."

She folded her hands and fought the need to lower her eyes. "About?"

He sighed. "Did you receive the checklist and the list of my expectations from Madame Eve?"

"Of course. Along with an application about as long as my arm. 1Night Stand is very thorough—even more thorough than the hoops I had to jump through to get my CPA license."

He chuckled. "A numbers gal, huh?"

"In the real world."

"Before we arrive at the resort, I'd like to discuss

some of things on your list." Opening his toy bag, he pulled out a familiar set of folded papers. "So if we do decide to...play afterward." He smoothed them open. "I see here, you have some experience with BDSM?"

"Several years. I made my first foray into the lifestyle during college."

"Of course, the time when many people explore their sexuality. My notes say you like bondage, some moderate pain, but no humiliation or bodily fluids? So you'd enjoy being strapped to the cross and letting me flog you?"

"Yes, Sir." Her nipples beaded against the tight bodice of her dress, and her panties grew damp.

His brows furrowed, jaw tight. "What about subspace?"

His words sent her desire crashing to the ground. Didn't he know the failure to find the hallowed place lay with her? He'd done everything he could to push her over the edge.

She licked her lower lip, unable to reveal she'd never found subspace, but unwilling to lie to him. "What of it?"

"Do you expect me to send you there?" He focused his piercing gaze on her. "Because I intend to. Nothing is more erotic for me than watching a woman completely submit to her needs. Knowing I've pushed her outside herself, until all she can do is float."

To hide her nerves, she twirled a long magenta lock of hair around her finger and winked at him. "Then I shall strive to give you what you want, Sir."

"I'm sure you will." He refolded the papers, shoving them back in the bag. "I am sure you will, but to ensure it I have two rules you must agree to before I will consent to play with you."

Akira's heart sank. She'd heard this speech before. *The same one he gave me in Chicago before we scened.* Somehow, she had to find a way past her authoritarian upbringing and be what Seba needed. She wanted those same things, even though it frightened her. She either rose to the challenge, or lost Seba forever. "Two rules, Sir?"

"You will not lie to me." His expression hardened. "Honesty between a Dom and his sub is essential." When she stiffened, he crossed his arms over his chest. "Look, I'm not trying to be some preachy asshole here. If something feels good, I want to hear it. Or if you need more—or less—of what I'm doing, you will open those pretty lips and tell me. I might not give it to you, but you will communicate with me. This leads to my second rule. There will be no hiding from me or the painful pleasure I need to give you. You've got to trust me to know how far to push, and when to back off. Do you understand?"

She swallowed hard. "Of course, Sir."

He gave a relieved sigh. "Good. Enough of the serious stuff. Tonight is supposed to be about relaxing and having fun. So, why don't you tell me a little bit about yourself—what are you like when you're not dressed up as the hottest manga character ever created?"

"Ordinary, quiet, reserved." She giggled. "It's all smoke and mirrors. Nothing more than fancy costuming and makeup. To label me sexy is a gift, Sir."

A grin tugged at his lips. "It looks like I'm going to have my work cut out for me tonight, because you, Mey-rin, are in no way, shape, or form ordinary."

"So, you dumped laundry soap in your father's

koi pond?" Seba chuckled.

Mey-rin shrugged, her cheeks pinking. "A harmless prank. I removed all the fish first. Still, my father didn't find it amusing. I ended up getting grounded for a month, but he never missed one of my dance recitals again."

"Sounds like you were a handful. Lord, if my brothers or I had done something like that, our dad would have tanned our hides."

"My father never hit me." She grew quiet, and her gaze seemed distant for a moment before she focused on him once more. "Let's say he had a different form of punishment." Her lips quirked. "He denied me things. If I couldn't act like a respectful *musume*, then I didn't eat with the family. If I flunked a test, I didn't get to walk in the garden after supper. He was very strict but quite fair."

Seba narrowed his eyes. Akira once said something similar about her father. Dread pooled in his stomach. *But she's in Chicago.* Still he stared at her in the dim light, trying in vain to find a clue that would convince him of her identity. But the opaque glasses she wore concealed most of her features. *Get over it. It's not her. Akira hates manga.*

"Sir?"

Mey-rin's soft, accented voice banished the thoughts of deception. Akira spoke flawless English. Mey-rin had a good command of the language, but the cadence of her birthplace rang in every word she spoke.

"Where in Japan did you grow up? My last submissive was from there as well."

She cocked her head and pursed her lips. "Are you accusing me of something, Sir? Believe it or not, Japan has a population of over 127 million people."

Before he could apologize, the phone next to him rang. Picking it up, he answered. "Hello?"

"Excuse me, sir. We'll soon be arriving at the resort." The chauffeur's soft voice filled his ear.

"Thank you." He eased the phone into its cradle before looking at Mey-rin. He wanted, no, he needed to rip the glasses away and see the color of her eyes. "Look, I didn't mean to accuse you of anything." He rubbed the back of his neck. "I'm a bit touchy tonight. I got cornered in the elevator by the girls from *Sailor Moon*."

She giggled. "Dear lord. I can't even begin to imagine your horror." Her laughter faded. "We all have baggage, Sir. Why don't we enjoy the masquerade and see where we are afterward. After too many fifty-to-sixty-hour weeks, I could use a bit of fun."

"You got a deal." He smiled at her, liking the lighthearted side he hadn't expected to see. "But you have to promise me a dance. It's been too long since I've twirled a woman in my arms."

She cocked her head. "I suppose so, but realize you're risking more than your toes. In that costume, I can't promise my hands won't wander. All those buttons make me want to open them with my teeth and lips...."

He groaned, the image of her undoing his clothing with her mouth popping into his brain. He narrowed his eyes but reined in the lust simmering just under the surface. "Naughty girls get spanked. Hard."

Her breath caught in her throat, but he could hear the need in her voice when she spoke. "Then I guess I'll have to be naughty."

Tempted to pull her over his lap, the only thing

saving her ass was the car coming to a stop. He yanked the zipper shut on his play bag. If he had his way, he'd have her bound to a St. Andrew's Cross wearing nothing more than her crisp white apron and begging for release before the end of the night.

As the door opened and she moved to exit, he took a deep breath. He needed to get a grip and quit acting like an over-eager teenaged boy. Grabbing his toy bag, he slid out of the limo and stopped to take in the resort. It looked almost like any other resort on the strip—opulent lights and sparkling glass except for the dark, almost forbidden vibe the gold trim and dark accents gave off. The building soared into the Vegas skyline, easily holding over a thousand rooms.

"Wow. Look at the size of this place. Maybe I should've had Wyk book a room here."

Next to him, Mey-rin stiffened. "Wyk?"

"My brother. He set up my travel arrangements, since I was out of town on business. But now I'm wondering if it wouldn't have been better to stay here." He placed his hand on her elbow, stifling his moan at the sight of the pebbled tips pressing against her silk top. "Time to go inside, before I do something we'll both enjoy."

"Sir?"

"Go." He leaned in and let his lips graze her ear. "Unless you want to find yourself up against the nearest wall with my mouth all over those pretty nipples you're teasing me with."

She shivered against him.

"Move," he ordered, hanging on to his control by a thread. He wasn't like this. The only other woman he'd ever reacted to was over seventeen hundred miles away. Guiding her to the door, he pushed her through it. When she swept past him, her hip brushed his groin. His cock throbbed in response as he trailed after her. Could it be his imagination, or had she deliberately added an extra sway to her walk?

A petite blonde, dressed in a long flowing white gown with gold accents and feathers in her hair, looked up when they approached. Stationed behind an ornate table outside the entrance to the ballroom, she greeted them. "Good evening, my name is Bonnie. Do you have your invitations?"

"Of course." Then Mey-rin about drove him around the bend, when she bent over to pull a folded form and invitation out of her thigh-high woolen stockings. He even caught a glimmer of the pistols strapped to her thighs, and he groaned.

Bonnie glanced up at Seba, a question in her eyes. "Sir?"

"I'm fine," he assured her.

"Good. Then may I take your bag for you, Mr. Michaelis?" Bonnie took his bag and tagged it before handing him his receipt and a small key. "This is yours. It will be stowed for safekeeping until after the masquerade."

"Thank you," he said.

"You're welcome." She winked at him then accepted the invitation Mey-rin held.

Bonnie scanned the back with a small handheld wand. The soft beep reached his ears. "You've read the rules?"

"Of course." Mey-rin's cheeks flushed.

"Good." Bonnie held out a small tablet. "Please initial the box, Miss Mey-rin, acknowledging you understand the rules concerning both the masquerade and the after party. Doing so will not constitute an agreement to play with any individual present."

Picking up the wand, Mey-rin held it over the tablet. "Too bad. I hear there are supposed to be some rather sexy individuals here tonight." She glanced over her shoulder and winked at him then turned back to scrawl her initials on the screen.

His blood raced south. *She can't possibly think I'm going to let her scene with another.* He caught her elbow, when she moved back.

Startled, she froze. "Sir?"

"The only person you'll be playing with tonight is me." He didn't bother to hide the lust in his words. The sooner she recognized he intended to claim her, the better.

A small grin tugged at her lips. "Perhaps, you can convince me...Sir."

Chapter Four

A kira caught her breath as she stood in the entryway of the ballroom. She hadn't expected the pure opulence surrounding her. She'd figured there would be polished wood floors, food, music, and dancing. Instead, the high-vaulted ceiling, with the etched marble under her feet gave the huge circular ballroom an airiness that belied its true size. Ice sculptures positioned around the room between each archway created a beautiful contrast to the white and black velvet draperies behind them. It was all so elegant, she felt out of place. Even the braided tassels of gold holding the heavy material open looked to be of the finest quality, and much too good for the likes of her.

Seba stopped next to her and gave a low whistle. "Damn, it looks like they spared no expense. Check out the table in the center. There are three champagne fountains." His fingers wrapped around her elbow. "Would you like something to drink? To settle your nerves before we mingle?"

She nodded. He knew her thoughts long before she could even voice them. Which was one reason the relationship's abrupt end had hurt so much—as if he'd seen something in her body language and found her lacking, not worth more effort. *But now is not the time to worry about things I can't change.*

The heat of Seba's hand burned her lower back

when he guided her through the crowd of costumed patrons. She bit her lower lip to keep from moaning at his touch. Classic rock poured from discreet speakers. A couple dressed as the Phantom of the Opera and his lovely Christine boogied by in a flurry of dark satin and white chiffon. Akira gaped after them. *No way can I dance like that.* "Unbelievable. I hope you don't expect me to gyrate all over the floor, Sir."

Seba chuckled then pulled her to the side to avoid a tall, muscular man in a white toga with a wreath of laurel around his head. With the dagger protruding from his side, she could only assume it was Julius Caesar or some other unfortunate Roman Emperor. Not that she'd ever seen a dead emperor doing the robot before.

"No, but I do hope we might have one slow dance later on." He placed himself between her and a server wearing black slacks and a gold-lame top, carrying a huge tray of finger sandwiches.

Finally, they arrived, without any collisions, to the sanctuary of the refreshment table.

Seba glanced around. "They're taking full advantage of the light and dark theme of the ball. Check out the beautiful virgin who just came in. Or should I say vixen." In a flowing, short white eyelet gown and ivory heels, with a pretty blindfold of uncut lace accentuating her long dark hair, the lady he referred to stood a few feet from the huge ice sculpture next to the entrance. A handsome blond man dressed as an archangel loomed over her. A few moments later, he moved away along the outer wall, while she headed in the opposite direction, toward the bathrooms.

"Beautiful," she agreed. "But, ten to one, he's not

her date. Someone as ripe for the plucking as she is would be more of a temptation for the devil himself than an angel." Arika waved toward a new arrival. "Like him."

Dressed in leathers and a long trench coat, with a red mask obscuring half of his face, the silver-haired man prowled across the floor with a predatory grace. "Doesn't he remind you of Faust? Ready to seduce his prey with worldly pleasures?"

Seba chuckled in her ear, surprising her with his closeness. Goose bumps raced up her spine. "I think you're a bit on the fanciful side, my dear Mey-rin." He nuzzled the flesh behind her ear. "But I'll take your bet. If he ends up with the virgin at the after party, I'll eat your pussy till you come at least three times...." He nibbled at her shoulder. "But, if I win, I want this"—he cupped her bottom, and she jumped, a whimper escaping her tight throat—"ass. Do you agree?"

Biting her lower lip, she wanted to press back against his hand, to beg him to do either. But that was what Akira would do, and tonight she wasn't her. For the next two hours, she would portray Mey-rin, a love-struck maid—trained lethal assassin by night, but a fumbling fool in the presence of her crush. So she took a shaky step away, catching herself on the edge of the lace and linen covered table. She turned to face him.

"You want to...."

He smiled, and one of those deadly dimples came to the fore, transforming him from a stern master into a seductive stranger. "What's wrong? Can't say the words, sweetheart?" He tipped her chin up with one finger. "It's real easy.... It's called ass fucking. Ever since you bent over to retrieve your invitation, all I've thought about is sinking deep inside your tight little bottom while you come against my fingers."

Her cheeks heated, much like her character's did in the presence of Sebby. Moisture flooded her panties at the erotic taunt. She dug her nails into her palms to keep from falling to her knees and baring her ass for him. While no stranger to anal sex, she had never experienced it with Seba. He'd used it as an incentive to reach subspace. *He claims nothing is more erotic than a sub allowing him to sink his cock into their asses, while they're floating high from the pleasured pain he's given them.*

"Nothing to say, my sweet Mey-rin?" He brushed his thumb over her cheek. "Or is it one of your darkest, hidden needs? To feel a thick cock stretching you there, until all you can do is moan?"

Biting her lower lip, she fought her rising tide of desire. She couldn't fall to his feet in a puddle of goo. She was made of sterner stuff. "Perhaps, before the night is over, you'll find out."

His eyes narrowed. "Are you challenging me?"

She shrugged then turned toward the fountain. Arching her back and thrusting her bottom toward him, she held first one then a second glass under the cascading cider. After both cups were filled, she bowed while offering him one. "We shall see. Us scening isn't a foregone conclusion, Sir. One of us may change our mind before the evening is over." She managed to take a single sip of the crisp beverage before he lifted the flute from her fingers and set it on the tray of a passing server.

"So we shall...but if I have a say, we will be. It'd be a shame to welsh on our wager."

She swallowed hard and cocked her head. "And

why's that?"

Taking her shoulders in his hands, he turned her to face the dancing couples. In the midst of the many costumed patrons, Faust glided with his virgin, his head bent close to hers. The solid outline of Seba's erection dug into her hip. Her former Master was still a very visual man, loving to watch the interaction between lovers. His openness about sex and his own needs had drawn her to him from the beginning.

"Because things are about to get interesting. Watch them...see how their bodies sway together, how the tension builds?" Seba lowered his voice, his tone a rough growl in her ear as he gathered her closer. "You're right about their attraction to one another. Lucky for you, because if the flush on her chest is any indication...I will look forward to spending some time feasting between your thighs."

He lifted her hand, and a sudden wet heat enveloped her fingers as he sucked them into his mouth then released them. A shiver worked up her spine when his breath, warm but cool against her damp skin, teased her. She bit back a moan at the sensation. Why did it always have to be this way? How could a mere brush of Seba Havas's body against hers make her want to melt into a puddle of goo?

He chuckled, and nuzzled her ear. "Perhaps I can even convince you to return the favor? I've thought of little else since the first time I saw your lips."

The little maid caught her breath, her body going almost limp against his. At her sharp inhalation, the soft mounds of her tits rose in an enticing manner. Naughty of him, perhaps, to tease her in such a way, but he couldn't resist. He needed her on the edge, so, when he ripped away the dark cloth, obscuring her soft curves from his view, she would beg for more.

Then I will find out how sensitive her nipples are, if they are a soft mocha or a delicious berry color. I want to devour them, and afterward use my favorite weighted clamps on the tips. But I must remember this isn't just about my wants. This is about sending Mey-rin outside of herself. To know I still haven't lost my touch.

"You did?" She looked up at him over her shoulder. Then her tongue skimmed her lips. It didn't take much on his part to imagine her on her knees in front of him, using those ruby lips on his dick.

"Of course, but I suspect you knew that. What woman wears ruby-red lipstick if it isn't to drive her date insane with lust? Now do we have a bet?" He pressed her back against his frame when the music swelled to a close. The deejay announced a short break, sending the crush of dancers stampeding toward the refreshment tables.

The need to reiterate the terms consumed her. "Quick recap. If you win...you get anal sex—"

He shook his head. "Not anal sex. Ass fucking. There's a difference, my sweet Mey-rin."

She flushed. "Fine. You win, I let you...fuck my ass, but if I win...you make me come?"

"Are you really that repressed?" He traced her collarbone. "If you win, I'm going to do more than make you come. I'm going to eat your tender little pussy until you can't see straight. Until you coat my face with your cream. Hell, at this moment, I don't know if I want to win or lose. So I guess we'll leave it up to our unknown friends. If you'll agree?"

A barely audible gasp escaped her. "Of course,

Sir. What a splendid way to predict the outcome of our first encounter."

Is the little vixen teasing or being sarcastic?

A minor commotion when the little flapper who'd taken their invitations trailed after a fast-moving Archangel Michael, distracted him from his thoughts. With his dark wings, brass chestplate, and dark leather war skirt, the fleeing man made quite an imposing figure. Then Faust broke away from his dark-haired virgin to join them. Interesting. How would this affect his bet with the delectable morsel in front of him?

"Well, that doesn't look good." Mey-rin dragged his attention away from the unfolding scene. "I hope whatever upset him won't reflect badly on the resort. Because, so far, everything has been top-notch."

"I'm sure it won't." Tucking her hand into the crook of his arm, he gave it a reassuring squeeze. "In the literature about tonight, I recall reading the owner of the resort commissioned the reclusive Arturo Bianchi to create a unique series of ice sculptures for this event. If I remember correctly, it's called the Journey of Submission. Shall we check them out?" He cocked his head. "Unless, of course, you'd prefer to eat or mingle with the rest of the guests?"

"I'd love to see the ice sculptures, Sir." She smiled up at him, her frilly maid's cap framing her face and several loose strands of burgundy-red hair.

Before the night's over, I will see the little bit of white frippery gone, along with those hideous glasses. She won't be able to hide forever. But first he had to tempt his delectable companion into playing with him. Their bet would be moot if she decided to end their date after the masquerade.

"Sir?" Her brow furrowed. "Have you changed your mind about seeing the sculptures?"

Shaking himself, he wrapped a hand around her hip and guided her toward the first of the sculptures. A small plaque at the base of the glistening art read, *Say Yes*, and featured two full figures. When they stopped in front of it, he hovered behind her so they almost mimicked the pose of the ice couple. The man stood behind a slender female, one arm wrapped around her waist, his head bent to her left ear. Seba could only imagine what the man was whispering in his prospective lover's ear. "Ah, the seduction. The sweet honeyed words a man says to convince the object of his affection that he's harmless." Seba placed his hands on her shoulders.

A giggle escaped her. "Sweet honeyed words?"

"Mmmm-hmmm." He pressed closer. "So I've been told. Too bad I suck at them."

"Aw, I'd say you're not doing too badly, Sir. At least a girl knows where she stands with you."

Seba froze, the words reminiscent of Akira. Had Madame Eve set him up with the one person he'd run over fifteen hundred miles to avoid?

He shrugged off the thought. "Why don't we see if any of the other statues are more appealing?" He straightened and guided her to the next one. Either she'd give herself away or prove his fear pointless. But heaven help her if she'd lied. When he said it was over, it was over.

"Of course, Sir." They made their away around the room, stopping at each ice sculpture. Not all featured a male Dom and female submissive. One showed a Domme with a male submissive bent over her legs, her hand forever poised in mid-swing.

Another depicted two males, with the dominant frozen in the act of flogging his submissive's broad back. They all intrigued her, but it was the final ice sculpture that truly called to her.

She stopped in front of it, her fingers curling up against her palms. The small plaque read, *Peace in His Embrace*. The name fit. The kneeling woman knelt between her Dom's spread thighs, her head resting against his knee and his fingers buried in her hair. The peaceful expression carved within the ice of both partners was nothing short of awe-inspiring.

That's what I want. To be so free nothing matters but him. No expectations, no disapproving looks...nothing but the peace that comes from knowing I'm safe and loved in his embrace.

"Beautiful, isn't it?" Seba's arm slid around her waist.

She nodded, unable to express how much she needed what the artist had captured in ice.

"It's what every Dom strives for. Nothing is more rewarding than knowing we've pushed our submissive outside herself, until she gives us everything she is." He pulled her back against him, and she savored the feel of his strong arms holding her to his chest. "And before the night is over, you will experience it—at my hands."

She drew a ragged breath. "I hope so, Sir."

Chapter Five

Over the next ninety minutes, Seba's promise rang in her ears. She couldn't forget the dark assurance in his voice, the solid feel of his body against hers, when he swore to give her what she needed. It didn't help every time his eyes met hers, she could see how much he wanted her at his mercy. Those fleeting touches weren't sufficient. She had a compulsion to be dominated—to prove she could, with her complete submission, give him whatever he needed.

But I have to wait. It's not time yet.

As she nibbled on finger sandwiches and petit fours, the music grew softer and the dancers began to dissipate. Soon the food was cleared away, until only the flowing fountains in the centers of the tables remained. A short time later, she noticed the wait staff had been replaced by dungeon monitors, whose gold corsets or vests over black leathers stood out in the crush of costumed patrons. The lights began to dim as two panels of the ceiling parted. Moonlight spilled down over the fountains, making them sparkle.

"My god." She gripped Seba's arm for balance while staring up at the gorgeous night sky. "How beautiful. I never expected there to be a skylight."

"Me either."

When she glanced over at him, she caught a

glimpse of movement. Two muscular dungeon monitors carried in a pair of small desks. The room grew quiet when they placed them at either side of the sensual ice sculpture that had captivated her longing earlier.

"Must almost be time for the after party to start." Seba nuzzled the top of her head. "Thank God. Please tell me you've decided to stay. I don't think I can wait any longer to play with this delicate body. You don't know how much—"

A buzz filled the room when a dark-haired man clad in black leathers, a studded harness crossed over his chest, and a floor-length black and red cloak, pushed through the crowd. Holding his hand, an ethereal blonde woman in a sheer white peignoir over a delicate lace halter and boy shorts, trailed after him.

"Good evening, ladies and gentlemen. Welcome to the grand opening of the Devil's Playground. I am your host for the evening, Asmodeus. As the Demon of Lust, appointed by the owners, my love and I have many treats in store for you."

Laughter erupted from the guests. Even Seba hooted. Obviously, everyone was ready to play.

"In fact, I do believe I will allow sweet Sarah to tell you more about our themed rooms. Just remember she's mine. If you have any nefarious intentions, I shall remind you it didn't end well for her past bridegrooms. The Demon of Lust keeps what is his."

Sarah rolled her eyes at his antics. "As my lord and master suggests, it will be my pleasure to tell you about the many accommodations awaiting your pleasure. Located through the various archways encircling the ballroom, each suite has its own private changing area and bathroom. These play areas can be reserved by the hour. Shortly, there will be DMs stationed at each archway." She rubbed her hand up and down Asmodeus's leather gauntlet. "I know I'm hoping Master will take me to the Medieval Torture Chamber."

Several people snickered.

"While there is a time limitation on the themed rooms, the main event of our night will be the opening of the Devil's Playground. Our newest dungeon has been designed for those who love to watch—and be watched. In a few minutes, DM's will man the desks behind me. Those who are submissive will register at the desk under the white curtain, while those who are dominant shall be directed to the black side. Please make sure you have your checklist available to register."

Akira cocked her head, looking over at the desks. She understood about registering—after all, the club needed to protect both itself and its patrons—but where the hell was the playground? Behind the men, black and white drapes framed an archway leading to a solid stone wall. She didn't see any openings. Seba nudged her forward. She flushed and whispered a sorry in his general direction. Leave it to her to be distracted by the mundane.

"The developers wanted a unique BDSM resort." Asmodeus made a wide gesture with one arm. "As you have noticed when you came in this evening, there are mineral springs, natural lighting, and in the early evening, we have a slight breeze which blows through, cooling not only the ballroom, but the other buildings as well. Above ground, the resort is an oasis, but below ground, it is entirely something else. Devil's Playground is a dungeon built into the side of an abandoned silver mine, forty feet underground, and, within the half hour, will be at your disposal. Everything needed to meet your darkest desires will be made available."

My darkest desires? Akira muffled her moan when images of long coiled whips, nipple clamps, and butt plugs filled her mind.

"Is there a problem, Mey-rin?" Seba wrapped a strong arm around her waist.

She shook her head, uncertain how to tell him the idea of baring her darkest desires in a dungeon buried beneath the earth felt liberating. Torn by her need to be honest and his touch, the rest of Asmodeus's speech barely registered.

"If an issue arises, find one of the dungeon monitors. While we want you to enjoy yourselves, we expect our club rules to be followed." He paused. "Other than that, have fun. Spank some ass and enjoy."

A low murmur of excited voices reached her ears as the crowd drifted in various directions.

Seba leaned closer, his body sheltering hers. "So what will it be, my sweet maid? A themed room, or will you take the chance and join me in the Devil's Playground?"

She chewed on her lower lip then ducked her head. "The Playground, Sir."

"Very good, Mey-rin." He tipped her head up and gently ran his finger down her cheek then over the spot pulsing under the skin of her throat. "Lose everything, but the glasses."

Her breath caught in her throat. "Sir?"

"In the changing room, you'll find a robe. I want you bare under it." He brushed his thumb over her lips. "Naked—except for the glasses."

She swallowed hard. "Of course, Sir."

***

Waiting at the end of the line, Seba struggled with the urge to push the other dominants aside. Several feet away, at the head of her own line, Mey-rin stepped up to the desk. He kept a close eye on her when she handed over her checklist then signed another electronic tablet. Against the zipper of his well-tailored butler's pants, his cock throbbed. He couldn't wait to have his luscious little maid strapped to either a cross or a bondage bed. To experience her cries of pleasure, as he used his favorite Gorean slave whip to pinken her creamy skin. It'd been so long since he'd had a willing submissive under his lash.

Since Akira.

He clenched his jaw, forcing thoughts of his last sub from his mind. He was *here* with Mey-rin. He shouldn't be thinking of another, especially when his date could give him what Akira had been unable to. When he stepped forward, Mey-rin skirted the table. A loud creak reached his ears, followed by a low groan of stone against stone. What he'd assumed to be a solid wall turned out to be the gateway to a tunnel. Akira slipped into the darkness. Before he could blink, the stone wall returned to its former position.

In front of him, a man dressed like the Phantom of the Opera whistled. "Damn, they're doing this to the hilt. Would you ever have guessed those walls were actual doors?"

Seba shook his head. "No. But nothing about this place has been what I suspected when I RSVP'd."

The Phantom arched a brow at him. "You mean when Madame Eve arranged it, right?"

A chuckle escaped Seba. "You got me there. Let me guess, you've used her services in the past?"

"Guilty. She paired me with my late wife, many years ago." The Phantom rolled his shoulders. A wave of melancholy seemed to pour off him. "It worked out so well, when our daughter threatened to hook me up with some dating site online, I told her I already had the perfect matchmaker. I contacted Madame Eve the very next day. I'm hoping she'll be able to work her magic a second time."

Seba scanned the immediate area. No one woman stood out as the love interest of the tortured Eric. "So your Christine is here somewhere?"

Hope filled his gaze. "I can only hope. Madame Eve assured me, I'd find her below."

"You're a more trusting soul than I. To go into a playroom filled with couples?" He shook his head. "I don't think I could do it. Ever since I un-collared my last sub, I've found it difficult to be around other couples—even in a play setting. Fortunately for me, I shared a limo ride with my date."

"So you got a jump start. I hope you've used it well." Eric pulled out a folded piece of paper. "All I have is this, and a vague promise of finding a dark-haired woman with a fair-skinned friend." He smoothed his fingers along the well-worn creases. It was almost as if he'd opened and folded the checklist several times.

"Well, I'm sure Madame Eve won't steer you wrong this time, either." He followed Eric when the line moved forward. "How long were you with your wife, if you don't mind my asking?"

"Sometimes it seems like forever, and other times not long enough." A rueful look crossed Eric's face—or what Seba could tell of it with the traditional white mask hiding half of the man's features. "Lord knows I loved her, even if I didn't always understand her." He looked up at Seba. "Want a friendly piece of advice? If your date isn't quite what she seems...don't let go. Don't give up. Hold her tight."

Before he could fathom what Eric meant by the cryptic words, they arrived at the front of the line. The Phantom turned and gave over his checklist. The DM studied it before handing it back. A quick scrawl on the tablet and Eric skirted the desk and strode through the now open door.

"Your checklist, sir?" The DM held his hand out.

After signing another waiver, Seba entered the dark tunnel lit by nothing more than torches hanging from stone holders. He walked carefully down the slanted hall until he came upon a well-lit plaque engraved with the word *Dominants* hanging next to a heavy oak door. Pushing against the thick surface, he slipped inside, expecting to be blinded by the light, but instead found a softly lit lounge. Overstuffed leather chairs positioned in a semicircle around the room welcomed a dominant to sit and rest, while the squat wooden tables separating them offered a place for their drinks. Several other Doms sat conversing about their plans for the evening. Behind them, a brighter light drew his attention. Another entryway led to a long bank of lockers, where he'd been assured his toy bag awaited him safe and sound, along with a change of clothing. While he'd loved roleplaying as Sebastian Michaelis, he was more than ready to don his leathers and once more be Master Seba. He needed to prove to himself Akira hadn't damaged him beyond repair.

It took him less than three minutes to find his locker. Placing the key in the lock, he opened it to find the familiar bag hanging from one side of the double hook. On the other hung a pair of leathers. Lifting them free, he looked for the tag. In the past, he'd had a bitch of a time finding a set that fit right. They usually had to be custom ordered. However, instead of a tag, he found, pinned to the waistband, another note from Madame Eve.

If you've come this far, I do hope you'll go a bit farther, my dear boy. Remember, a heart must be open to receive.
— Madame Eve

What was it with everyone telling or reminding him to cherish or be open to all the possibilities? Did they know something he didn't? Well, other than the identity of his date? Deciding it didn't matter, he shed his costume and slipped into his leathers. A perfect fit. He should've expected nothing less, considering the high quality of the costume Madame Eve had sent him. Shutting the locker, he locked it. He'd need his costume later because he'd be damned if he left the club to go back to the hotel in nothing more than a set of tight leathers. Not with a crazy sci-fi convention going on. His luck, he'd get stuck in the elevator with a bunch of horny ewoks or something.

Taking a quick glance in one of the full-length mirrors at the end of the lockers, he grabbed his bag from the bench, hefted it over his shoulder, and left the changing room. The need to play rode him hard as he stalked down the ramp toward the Devil's

Playground.

The moment he passed through the entry, hard-driving rock music hit him. At the same time, he spotted a slender, ivory-skinned woman wearing nothing more than a transparent peach-colored robe. She stood with her back to him next to the DM station a few yards away.

Akira.

Only one woman sported the gorgeous tattoo he'd traced with both his whip and tongue. When she shrugged at whatever the DM told her, the muscle along her shoulder flexed, causing the petite hummingbird to dip its beak into the lush lotus flower. His dick hardened at the tantalizing sight, even as anger spiked through him.

Akira! What the hell is she doing here?

Forgetting all about his waiting playmate, Seba stalked across the room, ready to give Akira a piece of his mind. How dare she interrupt his date? But before he'd covered the distance between them, she turned to face him. He froze in shock. Perching on her slightly upturned nose were Mey-rin's opaque glasses. Suddenly, the reasoning behind the note made sense, even if he had no intention of accepting the matchmaker's advice.

Then Mey-rin...or, rather, Akira spotted him. Her lips slowly parted then drew up into a gorgeous smile. The skin at the corner of her eyes crinkled as she took a step toward him. Her happiness at seeing him seemed to spread until it engulfed her petite frame. He swallowed hard, torn between leaving and demanding a full refund from the elusive Madame Eve, and staying and taking what Akira offered—until he fucked her out of his system. But before he could decide on which course of action to take, his former submissive came to a stop in front of him and sank to her knees, head bowed.

"I offer my body to you willingly, Sir. To whip or fuck. I am at your service. I only wish to please you."

A low growl built in him. She'd pressed every one of his erotic buttons with her words. An offer she had made many times in the past, but always failed to follow through on.

"Look at me, *kotori*." The endearment rolled off his tongue.

At his feet, she stiffened. But it no longer mattered. She'd seen his face, knew his identity, what he was capable of, and had still offered herself. When she lifted her head, he took the glasses off, confirming his suspicion. Her beautiful golden-brown eyes stared up at him, the longing in their depths familiar.

"There will be no way out this time. At least, not tonight. You will submit because I will accept nothing less than a total sacrifice on your part. Do you understand?"

Chapter Six

Akira wondered if she should be worried. Heated desire mixed with anger in his eyes. He wanted her despite his anger about her deception. Because she lied or because he hadn't expected her to be his date? She didn't care. She'd have to work past either or both before the night was through.

"I asked you a question, Akira. I expect an answer." Ice dripped from his words.

She ran her tongue over her lower lip. "Complete submission, total sacrifice, *Sensei.*"

His eyes narrowed in irritation at her address, he drove his fingers into her burgundy hair jerking her head back.

She winced at the sting, but accepted it as her due. In the limo, he'd warned her about the honorific. About how she had hidden behind it in the past, and how he wouldn't tolerate her using it tonight.

"What did you call me?" His sharp tone raked over her.

"Old habits die hard...Sir. I'll strive to remember. Things will be different this time."

"Damn right they will be. You want to know why?" He leaned in until his nose was inches from hers. "Because the next time it comes out of your mouth, it will halt everything. We'll be done." He smirked. "Think of it is as your new safeword."

Akira's heart pounded in her ears. He'd stripped away her last shield. She was vulnerable in a way she'd never been before. Like a child whose parent had taken away her security blanket for her own good. Like said child, she wanted to plead with him to give it back. But the firm set of his lips and heavy lowering of his brows told her no plea would change his mind. Would she accept the inevitable, or walk away?

I'm not walking away.

"*Sensei* it is, Sir."

His hold on her hair loosened, and he stepped back. "Good." He glanced over his shoulder. "I want you up there."

Her knees wobbled. A St. Andrew's Cross on an elevated dais dominated the center of the room. The dark wood gleamed in the flickering light from the torches situated on the walls.

"You're going to strip off your robe and climb the dais. Then you will stand at ease in front of the cross. Understand?"

"Yes, Sir." Her hands reached for the tie on her robe as she searched for a way to the platform. *This is it. There will be no going back this time.* She'd sacrifice all on the altar of his lust. Her desire to surrender surpassed her terror.

The stone stairs on the back of the dais were cool against her bare feet. Arriving at the top, she dropped the robe. Her throat dried when she glanced over her shoulder. Amphitheater-style stone benches, fitted with thick pillows rose well above the sandy, stone floor of the Devil's Playground. Whoever sat there would have a perfect and rather intimate view of any scene taking place on the dais. A trickle of moisture streaked down her leg. Every Dom and sub in the playground would watch Seba conquer her.

"I thought I asked you to wait at the cross." Seba's brisk tone had her swallowing hard.

"The crowd, Sir...."

Doms settled in their seats, their subs either curled on their laps or next to them.

"Think of yourself as a wet, spicy, morsel to whet their appetite." Seba moved closer to her. "Imagine what it will feel like when I send you into subspace with all those greedy eyes watching?"

She caught the "Sensei" before it passed her lips. "S-s-sir?"

"But we have the matter of your disobedience to deal with first. I believe I asked you to be waiting at the cross, not gawking at our observers."

"Yes, Sir." She moved toward the cross. A muted thud of a bag hitting the dais floor followed her. But before she made it to her destination, he ordered her to stop. Trembling with anticipation, she froze in place.

"Since you won our bet, I guess I'll have to be satisfied with filling your pretty ass with this." Seba opened his bag and withdrew a silicone butt plug.

Her heart leapt at the familiar toy. More than once he'd spread her open, tied her to the cross, then plugged her tight ass. *Making me ready for his cock.* Then his words registered. "Bet, Sir?"

She followed his gaze to where a tall, silver-haired man wearing leathers strapped his submissive, a naked brunette with long curls spilling over her shoulders, into a pair of the manacles hanging from the stone wall. "Don't they look a lot like our Faust and Virgin?"

Her thighs clenched in reaction, and her nipples tightened when the reality of what she witnessed registered. "Yes, Sir."

He chuckled. "Which means, before the night is through, I'm going to feast on your pussy, Akira." He nipped her bare shoulder. "And there will be nothing you can do but take every lash of my tongue and scrape of my teeth."

Her breath caught on a soft moan.

"Now, bend over and present that ass for me."

She leaned forward, wrapping her fingers around the left support of the cross.

"Damn, still beautiful." Seba accented his compliment with a sharp slap to her ass.

Pain washed through her, only to morph into pleasure when he thrust his fingers inside her sheath. It was always like this.

Always.

"And wet." He withdrew to smear her cream over her anus.

She gasped. His touch against such a sensitive place had her trembling with anticipation. She pushed back against his fingers.

"Ever the eager little *kotori*." Seba pulled back, only to thrust his fingers inside her dripping folds once more. "Be still," he ordered when she tried to ride their thick lengths.

"Sorry, Sir." She struggled, but obeyed. It was hard. She wanted more.

A low snick signaled the drip of cool lube against her rosette. He curled his fingers and pressed against her G-spot. Pleasure struck hard, along with the need to rock against them.

"Shhh...relax for me." Then the plug's narrow tip breached her.

She gritted her teeth and pushed out, eager for the penetration.

"Good girl, let me in." With slow movements, he fed the plug into her ass, each thrust stretching and burning anew, until she wanted to scream at him to let her come.

***

Seba growled when Akira's pussy clamped down on his fingers. Hard to believe with such little play—a little fingering, a whole lot of dirty talk, and she was already on the verge of coming.

Always like this.

It made him want to forgo the punishment, screw the whipping he had planned, and bury his cock in her tight little ass. He might have lost the bet, but before they left, he'd find out how tightly her ass would grip him. It might be the last chance he got.

At the sobering thought, he jerked his fingers free of their warm prison. The muscles in her thighs trembling against his hand.

"Not yet, *kotori*. Stand up. I have a few things left before I restrain you to the cross." Turning, he rummaged in his bag for the nipple clamps and gold chain he'd brought with him. "Face me, arms behind your head."

He tested the clamps on his pinky as she obeyed, checking to make sure they were working properly then moved toward his sub. Her flushed face showed no fear. Her erect nipples taunted him. He longed to tongue—tease them. He could easily clamp their tight peaks but found himself unable to resist the pear-shaped mounds topped with their light-brown tips.

Leaning in, he cupped one breast and sucked hard on the nipple. Akira whimpered, but he paused. Familiar steps to an old routine. He released her with a loud pop, irritated. What he'd tried in the past hadn't worked. He needed something different to keep her off-balance. He stepped back. "Hold."

"Yes, Sir?"

He ignored her question. She was his to do with as he pleased, the conditions of their evening set in the great deal of forms filled out for 1Night Stand and filed with the DMs before their descent into the dungeon. Running over Akira's hard and soft limits, he got an idea. One he'd never considered before, but with only one night together, desperation drove him. The man he'd spoken with earlier, the widower, stood alone near the door to the aftercare rooms. Seba descended the staircase and approached him.

"Eric, right?" Seba eyed his downcast expression. "Still waiting for your date?"

The tall blond shrugged, his jaw tense. "I was, but an unexpected issue caused my Christine not to show. I just got a text from Madame Eve. Something about my date's plane being delayed. I guess we're going to have dinner tomorrow night."

He'd guessed the man had been stood up and saw an opportunity to brighten both their nights. "Since you have the evening free, would you care to help me with my sub? She has a serious issue in letting go. Maybe, between the two of us, we'll be able to convince her otherwise?"

Erik looked up at the raised dais then back at Seba. "Are you sure you want to share her with me? You don't know me from Adam."

Seba clapped him on the shoulder. "You passed Madame Eve's background check, and that's all I need to know."

"What exactly is your plan?" Eric looked skeptical. "I don't do blood, fire, or breath play."

Seba grinned. "A good old-fashioned whipping, along with all the stimulation we can give her. My *kotori* has a high pain threshold, and while I won't deliberately break her skin, I'll make her wish I had. I need you to keep her off-balance. I'm hoping your presence will push her past whatever is holding her back."

Eric looked doubtful. "And you got all that from the checklist Madame Eve had us fill out?"

"Akira and I have a past. Back in Chicago, I specialized in abused and troubled subs. Those who struggled with the lifestyle but were still determined to participate. Akira could not achieve subspace, could never completely submit." He glanced at her. "She's my one failure. A sub I had to walk away from. Madame Eve, in her infinite wisdom, gave me a second chance to get this right, and damned if I'm gonna let it slip through my fingers."

Understanding dawned in Eric's gaze. Finally, he nodded. "I'm all for second chances. Let's do it."

Relief poured through Seba. For a moment, he'd thought Eric would refuse. "Thanks. When we get up to the dais, I want you to clamp those pretty little nipples of hers. Then I will secure her to the cross, but I need you to hook the nipple chain I brought with me around it so you can stand behind the cross and tug on it. Any questions?"

"Yeah, what are you going to be doing while I torment your little sub's nipples?"

A wide grin crossed Seba's face then he lifted the Gorean slave whip from his belt. "I'm going to make her dance under this. We're going to strip away her control one layer at a time. We'll find out why she can't let go."

"And when we do?" Eric studied him.

"Then we'll push her over the edge."

A slow grin crossed Eric's face. "And what's in it for me? Other than watching your pretty little sub submit?"

"What do you want? If it's to fuck her, I'm sorry. I never share my subs that way. It's also a hard limit for my sub, but one of Akira's fantasies has always been to have another man come all over her while I claim her."

"Jerk off on a willing sub? I can deal with that. Besides, scening with a couple beats a lonely jerk-off session back at the hotel."

Akira panicked and almost dropped her arms when the blond Dom followed Seba back up the steps. *What the hell is he doing?* She chewed on her lower lip. Seba came to a stop in front of her, lifting her chin to stare down at her.

"Do you trust me—knowing that I'll never cross your hard limits, Akira?"

She swallowed hard. The determined lust stamped across his face scared her, especially after his earlier anger, but it stoked her desire higher. The potent combination made her heart race until she felt like a mouse about to be swooped up by a falcon.

She hesitated for a moment then answered. "Of course, Sir."

Pleasure flitted across his expression, giving her an almost euphoric feeling. "Master Eric is going to assist me tonight. You will treat him as you would me. If he asks you a question, I expect you to answer honestly. No evasion, no hiding, understand?"

"Yes, Sir."

"Good." He stepped back and waved to Master

Eric. "She's all yours."

Her heart leapt into her throat. She'd thought Seba was tall, but the blond towered over her Master. Her head didn't even come up to his sternum. Seba expected her to submit to a stranger?

"Relax, little one." Eric traced a finger over her cheek and down her collarbone. "I won't break you. I'm here to help."

Already primed from Seba's earlier play, her nipple tightened further when Eric lightly brushed over the distended peak.

She gasped when he brought his other thumb into play. "Help with what, Master Eric?"

"Why, nothing less than driving you insane." He gave her a wicked grin then held up a clamp and slipped it onto her taut nipple.

She gave a squeak at the pinch then breathed through the sting.

"Good girl. You didn't even drop your arms." Master Eric's words bolstered her confidence as a sub.

She opened her mouth to thank him, but he brushed his lips over her hair before clamping the opposite nipple. Seba took his place in front of her. "Damn, I love seeing your pretty little nipples like this, *kotori*." He reached out and flicked the small weights.

The dull ache jolted through her but settled like a warm hand over her womb. She gasped in reaction. *"Sir...."*

"Talk to me. Tell me what you want."

She bit her lower lip but forced herself to talk. This time had to be different, or she'd lose him—this time forever. "I need more. Harder, please. Make my nipples ache."

Seba's nostrils flared as he grasped the weights between his thumbs and forefingers. Then he lifted them, tugging firmly.

Pain shot from her abused nipples down to her clit, causing her sheath to clench as her ass squeezed the plug. She cried out in pleasure.

"I bet I could make you come from just this." Seba pulled up again, sending another burst of pleasured pain through her. "But I'm not going to. You're not going to get off that easily tonight." He released the weights. "In fact, it's time for your whipping. To the cross."

With thighs slicker than she could ever remember them being, she obeyed.

Chapter Seven

Stepping back, Seba eyed the exquisite banquet laid out in front of him. With both arms stretched up and secured by soft leather cuffs at the top of the X, Akira lounged with her chest against the slightly tilted St. Andrew's Cross. Eric looped the chain around the wood then secured it to the weighted clamps. Lust shot straight to Seba's groin when the other Dom winked at him then tugged on the gold links and Akira moaned softly.

"Like that, sweetheart?" Eric continued to toy with the chain.

"Yes, Master Eric."

"Good, then I'll make sure to do it often." He eyed Seba. "Or perhaps more, if you give us the answers we seek."

"Oh, my God," she whispered.

Unhooking the Gorean slave whip from his waist, he swung it a few times, warming up his right arm. The five long falls, a yard in length and an inch and a half in width, whistled as they cut the air.

Akira tilted her head at the sound. Even restrained, she attempted to identify which toy he had. "Sir?"

Of all of his whips, floggers, and crops, she'd worshipped this toy, but feared it the most. He could understand why. In an inexperienced hand, the heavy-impact toy could do a tremendous amount of damage. But, as she knew, he wielded the leather with an expertise that had many subs begging to feel its kiss.

"Yes, *kotori*?" He shifted the whip to his other hand, warming up his left arm. Being ambidextrous, he often took advantage of the talent for the benefit of the lucky sub who ended up under his lash.

"Are you going to use the kurt, Sir?"

"Does the idea of your master using such a heavy toy against your lily-white skin make your pussy wet, sub?"

Seba paused mid-swing, expecting Akira to deny it. She never gave in easily.

"I...yes." Her head dropped between her arms, only to be jerked up as Eric gave a harsh yank on the stretched chain.

"What's the second rule, sub?" Eric's stern tone even had Seba grimacing. The man wasn't playing around.

Akira gasped. "No hiding."

"Then why did you?" Eric's face became a sadistic mask. "Unless, of course, you wish for the pain?"

She shook her head. "No, Master Eric. I slipped. As a child, I suffered many years of training not to look those above me in the eye. But I understand I am not to hide. It won't happen again."

Jealousy warred with relief. His *kotori* was opening up, and even if it was to another Dom, he should be happy.

But I'm not.

He clenched his jaw and reminded himself to keep his eye on the prize: sending Akira into subspace. If it took both him and Eric to do it, so be it.

"Then answer the question, Akira." Seba stepped closer, stroking the weighted handle down her spine. "Would the idea of me marking your beautiful skin with my wicked toy have you ready to cream your panties...if you had any on?"

She arched against the stroke of the handle. "Yes, Sir." A shiver wracked her body when he tossed the whip at her shoulder, trailing the falls across her soft skin. "Even as it scares me, I find its fierce kiss to be very arousing."

"It's like being attracted to a man twice your size—he could hurt you with his strength, but you trust him not to." He caressed her lower back with the strands of the whip. "Isn't that what you once claimed when I asked why you'd chosen me over the other Doms at LRA?"

"Yes, Sir." Her hips shifted toward him when he teased the tempting rise of her ass with the leather. Her eagerness sent a surge of lust through him.

"What is your safeword?"

"*Sensei,* Sir." Anticipation filled Akira's response.

"Good. What level are you at?" He moved back several feet from the cross.

"Green, Sir."

"Count off." He drew his arm back and struck her left shoulder at about quarter strength. A faint mark appeared.

"One, Sir," she moaned.

The next blow landed a few inches below the first. Jerking against her restraints, she called out the number.

Meeting Eric's eyes, he mouthed the words *warm up* as he littered her back with short, but thuddy, strokes. When her skin took on a light-pink hue, he paused. "What level are you at, *kotori?*"

"Green, Sir," she answered in a surprisingly strong voice.

"Good, now the fun can begin. Eric, if you please?"

Master Eric pulled up a bit harder on the chain, tugging at her captured nipples, and Akira hissed. The pain morphed into pleasure when he eased off a bit and returned the dangle to its former position. She relaxed for a moment, only to gasp as he tortured her poor nipples in a random pattern. Without warning, her back lit up. She grunted, swaying forward at the impact. He'd been taking it easier on her earlier. The kiss of leather against her upper back alternating down to her ass left a fiery path of brutal sensation. How such pain could bring her such fierce pleasure, she didn't know.

Good girls are pure. They don't give into the temptations of the flesh, Akira. Her father's voice tried to intrude in her pleasure.

"Focus on me, Akira," Master Eric coaxed, yanking on the chain.

"Yes, Master Eric."

His blue eyes crinkled at the corners. "Good girl. Don't let whatever is torturing you win."

She gritted her teeth. Another lash landed on the middle of her back then wrapped around her side. "Like Sir isn't...." She tried for humor, but failed as another blow, this one on her opposite side, sent a new flood of lust pooling in her pussy.

"And like you're not enjoying every minute of it, my *kotori*." Seba taunted.

She arched when one particular blow struck where her thigh joined her ass. "God, yes!"

The pain blended with the coaxing words of Master Eric and the crooning ones of her Sir, as they both praised her ability to take his lash. Just as she hovered on the edge of floating free, her father's face appeared before her.

"No, Father," she cried out. He had no place in this. She had to prove to Sir she could do this. She must not give into her father's influence yet again.

"Stay with us, Akira." Eric's voice came from far away, but his sharp jerk on the nipple chain cut through her father's image like a hot knife through butter.

"Don't let him win. Nothing you're doing here is wrong. Your father has no place in our pleasure." Seba's voice grounded her, brought her back to the moment.

Pain radiated from her nipples. She groaned, her eyes opening to focus on Eric's face. *He isn't my Master, he shouldn't care one way or another if I let go.* She glanced away.

"No." The harsh bark from Seba, followed by a harder, stronger blow to her already warmed ass had her jerking in both surprise and pain.

"Sir's mad," she murmured in distress.

"No, he's not mad, sweetheart. At least, not at you." Eric cradled her cheek with his free hand. "He's angry at whatever is keeping you from taking what you need. Let it go."

"I can't," she whispered, beyond mere fear that no matter how much she wanted what the men offered her, the potent, compelling conditioning her father had instilled in her from birth would never let her find the ultimate release.

"Yes, you can." Eric looked into her eyes. "Focus on the lash. How does it feel?"

She blinked at him. "Like the wind coming off Lake Michigan during a thunderstorm. Sharp, almost pelleting, but breathtaking at the same time." She groaned when the lash found the side of her breast. "The sharp, crisp, edge of pain is followed by warmth—pleasure that bursts over me like the soothing jets of a whirlpool."

"Good," Seba said. "Remember that. Imagine standing on Navy Pier before a storm, seeing the clouds roll in and the exhilaration you feel.... Go there any time your father tries to butt into something which is none of his business."

She groaned again as Eric tugged on the chain, adding another layer of sensation. It pushed her until she floated, tethered only to the Doms working so hard to push her into subspace.

Good girls don't let men tie them to crosses and whip them in public for their sexual edification. You're a disgrace to the Ito name.

She cried out in frustration. Tears washed down her cheeks. She couldn't do it. "No...."

"We got to switch." Eric raked a hand through his hair. "She's so close, but she needs an extra shove. She needs you."

"Fuck." Seba handed his whip to the other man. "Ever handle one of these before?"

Eric took it. "Yes, quite often. My wife enjoyed the bite."

"Good. Keep it at a steady pace...but avoid her shoulders. I've already given them quite a workout."

"No problem." He grabbed Seba's arm. "Just don't let her retreat. We've worked so hard—"

"I won't. She finally gave me the key to her

reticence. Her father." Seba moved to the front of the cross. It suddenly made sense. Akira had said her upbringing had been strict. But the idea she'd let it influence her to the point she couldn't let go, pissed him off.

Moving so he stood in front of her, he grasped the chain. "Look at me, *kotori*."

Her dazed eyes landed on him. "Sir?"

"Focus on me." He yanked on the chain, pulling her nipples out instead of up. "Repeat after me...my father is a bastard and has no place in Sir's and my pleasure."

"My...father...is—"

Eric lashed her buttocks, and she jerked.

"Finish it." His tone was harsh, but he didn't care.

"Is...a bastard...and has...."—she winced when he gave her nipples another tug—"has no place in...Sir's and...my pleasure...." Tears sparkled on her lashes.

"Again," he ordered.

She mumbled the words, her gaze losing some of its sharpness.

"Again." He leaned in, his face only inches from hers.

"My father is a...bastard...and has...no place in Sir's...and my pleasure." Her response strong despite its dreaminess.

"Good girl. Now, let go for me. I'll catch you."

"You will?" The hesitancy in her voice about killed him.

"Yes, and when I do, I'll eat your pussy for hours."

Her tongue darted out. "Want the other...." she mumbled.

"Other?" He cupped her chin.

"My ass...I need you to fuck...it...please, Sir. I've been good." With a cry, she slumped forward.

His cock nearly exploded. "Son of a bitch."

Akira was floating along when the thuds of the whip stopped, replaced instead by the warmth of her Sir's body. She gave a soft mewl of pleasure as he toyed with the plug in her ass.

"That's it. Fly high for me, *kotori*." The hard edge to his voice broke through the lovely peace she'd found.

"Wha...?" she mumbled.

"Shh, everything is all right. Don't tense. I want to feel that pliant pussy around my cock."

Her Sir's raw need and the thick erection wedged against her sore ass tugged her back to reality.

"She's coming back to us." Eric's voice seemed loud.

She opened her eyes. "Wow."

"Wow is right." Eric rubbed his hand over the tented crotch of his trousers. "I don't think I've ever witnessed a sub fly so high. You're damned lucky your master has a rule about you fucking others. I'm so damned hard I could split wood."

She licked her lips. "Let me see, Master Eric?"

"Go ahead. Let her see." Seba lifted one of her now freed legs and thrust his condom-sheathed cock deep inside her pussy, stretching her.

Pleasure threatened to sweep her away. But she wanted what he'd promised...his cock in her ass. "Sir!"

"Relax, Akira. Watch Master Eric. See how he's stroking his cock? You did that. You made him hard."

She moaned as Eric wrapped his fist around the

thick length of his dick, before measuring the length of it from its ruddy tip to the soft blond pubes at its base. "Oh God. It's huge."

"I'll take that as a compliment," Eric croaked out. "Fuck...I ache." A rueful smile crossed his face. "It won't take long."

"Hold off, at least until I get in her ass."

She cried out when he withdrew from her pussy. Then his fingers plucked the plug out of her ass. She felt so empty! But not for long. She pressed back to meet the broad tip of Seba's lubed cock. She tried to relax so it could push past the slight resistance at her anal ring.

"Sir!" She tossed her head back.

"Fucking tight." His fingers dug into her hips, steadying her. "You can come whenever you want— often as you want, *kotori*. In fact, the crowd would be very disappointed if you didn't."

The reminder of their curious, interested audience registered as he snapped his hips, each thrust jarring her forward. She squealed at the sheer eroticism of it all. She didn't know what pushed her higher: her Sir fucking her ass, Master Eric jerking off, or the approval given by the presence of others. She cried out. Her first orgasm raced toward her.

"Shit...gonna come." A grimace creased Eric's face.

"Come on me," she begged.

"Fuck yeah." Stepping forward and to the side, he let go with a roar, his seed coating the left side of her body.

With each drop that hit her, the coil inside her tightened. Then Sir plunged his fingers into her sopping pussy, filling her with three while his palm rotated against her clit. She came on a scream.

"Good girl," Seba gritted out between clenched teeth as his own release wracked his body.

As she floated back down from her orgasm, Akira mourned the absence of his seed. If this was to be her only time with Seba, she wanted to be marked in an elemental way. A lone tear escaped to roll down her cheek when he withdrew from her body.

"Shhh, don't cry. Everything is all right." Seba freed her from the cross, cradling her against his chest. "Can you clean up then bring my toys to the aftercare room, Eric?" He scooped her up and carried her down the steps.

Epilogue

"Sir!" The plea escaped Akira's throat as Seba lashed at her clit with his tongue. Back at the Castillo Hotel and Resort, Seba seemed determined to drive her insane with pleasure. With her hands tied to the headboard, she could do nothing but plead with him. Sprawled on his stomach between her thighs, he feasted on her pussy. It all seemed surreal. She'd expected at best to curl up in his arms before sleeping, or, at worst, a good-bye kiss from him at her door before he returned to his own room. Her fantasies did not include this devouring. Nothing had prepared her for the pleasurable torture raining down on her tender sex.

"Mmmm," he mumbled, slipping a finger in her pussy and another in her ass.

She screamed, as she convulsed once more. Riding out the pleasure, she became aware of Seba scrambling to his knees between her wide-spread thighs.

"Mine." His fierce expression, his lips coated with her juices, as he cupped her ass in his hands, left little room for doubt. He joined their bodies with a single hard thrust.

The pleasure, which had been ebbing away, returned twofold, battering her. So intense, it scared her, and she began to struggle against her bonds. But her Sir's hoarse but firm voice cut through her panic.

"Relax into it." He gave a languid twist of his hips. "I've got you."

She whimpered, but obeyed.

"Good girl. You deserve a reward." His hand slipped between their bodies.

"No...." Her protest ended in a groan when his thumb found her clit. Pleasure swamped her once more.

"Fuck yeah! Come all over my cock." A bead of sweat coursed down the side of his face. He hooked her legs over the crooks of his arms and covered her body with his, thrusting slowly and impossibly deep. "Prove you're mine, Akira."

With a shattered cry, she slipped over the edge of subspace.

***

The next morning, Seba woke alone. Patting the bed next to him, he frowned. Where had she gone? Fear coursed through him. *She's mine, and I'll be damned if I let her go.* Sometime between their third and fourth loving, he'd realized he'd be a fool if he gave up the little submissive who held his heart in her small hands.

"Akira!" He pushed back the blankets and swung his legs over the side of the bed.

She appeared in the doorway wearing nothing but the translucent peach robe and carrying a tray of steaming food.

"Morning, Sir." Her cheeks flushed, she approached the bed. "If you'll sit back...." She held up the tray. After arranging himself against the headboard, she set the tray across his lap. "Breakfast is served." She lifted the lids off the dishes. The savory aromas of biscuits and sausage gravy teased his nose.

His stomach grumbled, and Akira giggled. "Eat. I'm going to shower."

He wanted to protest, but she disappeared into the bathroom. Deciding he'd have plenty of time to discuss her collaring when she came out, he dug into the delicious food.

He was wiping his mouth with his napkin when the door reopened, and Akira walked out in a pair of distressed jeans and a pretty coral sweater with her magenta-dyed hair piled on top of her head. She even had her shoes on.

"Why did you get dressed? I thought we could spend the day exploring each other in bed."

A sad look crossed her face. "Let's not make this any harder than it needs to be, Sir. You gave me a memorable night, but it's over."

He shoved the tray off his lap, uncaring if the dirty dishes spilled on the bedding. "What do you mean it's over?"

"Our agreement was for last night alone. I didn't expect to share your bed, so I thank you for the gift. However, as magnificent as it was, I need to go home. Master Randy is waiting for my answer."

"What answer?" He surged off the bed.

Uncertainty flickered in her eyes. "About whether or not I want to be his submissive."

"Then you have a problem. You're *my* submissive." He jerked her against him.

"I *was,* but you un-collared me." She pulled away from him. "So it's time to let me go, Sir."

"Hell fucking no." Desperation started to creep up on him. He'd never expected her to walk away from him. Not after all she went through to get back with him.

"You have to." She looked up at him. "While last night was phenomenal, I can't continue to give you everything when I know I'm nothing more than a pleasurable pastime." She pressed her hand against his chest. "My heart can't take it."

Seeing an opening, he lunged at it. "Good, because mine can't take seeing you with another man." He cupped her cheek. "I love you, Akira."

"You do?" Hope filled her voice.

"Of course. Like a thief in the night, you stole my heart the first time you offered yourself to me. Why else do you think I went on that damned date? I couldn't go to my club because I couldn't bear to see you with another, nor could I find pleasure with another submissive if you were there."

She gave a watery chuckle. "Do you know how hard it was to scene with Randy?" She pressed her face against his chest. "I did even worse with him than I did with you...and this time, it wasn't because my father's damned morals kept creeping in." She brushed a kiss over his heart. "He could never be you."

"Of course he can't be." He tipped her head up. "Stay with me. I didn't bring your collar with me, but it's at home—just waiting for you."

"If you're sure?" Tears sparkled on her lashes, but she grinned up at him.

"I'm more than sure." He lifted her off her feet. "In fact, I'll prove it right now." He tossed her on the bed then crawled on top of her. Her long hair came loose and splayed over the pillow in shining waves. "I wonder how many times I can make you come before I remove all of your clothing."

She giggled, tugging him down into her arms. "I'm sure we'll find out, *Sensei*."

"Damned straight." He growled, nosing aside her hair and nibbling her neck. "And after that, you're going to call Venus and tell her Madame Eve has struck again. Tell her she and my brother are to spread the word you're taken. Understand?"

"Yes, *Sensei*."

The End

About Dakota Trace

Dakota is a simple Midwest girl, who has found her passion in storytelling at a young age. Her father was always saying she was making up the craziest stories. Most remained unwritten though as writing wasn't Dakota's strong suit. That all changed in junior high when she took her first typing class. Problem solved for the dyslexic Dakota. There was no stopping her after that.

She wrote her first novel her freshman year on an old electric IBM typewriter. The story was about a girl who could speak to animals. And Dakota never looked back.

Writing in several different genres, she is now a published author with multiple books under her belt. When she isn't writing, she's a crazy mom of three wild Indians who are posing as children.

To find out more about Dakota, visit her at: www.DakotaTrace.net.

To sign up for Dakota's newsletter go to: https://secure.campaigner.com/CSB/Public/Form.aspx?fid=658095

www.ingramcontent.com/pod-product-compliance
Lightning Source LLC
Chambersburg PA
CBHW071520170626
46811CB00007B/2912